"So, you at least have some faith in me."

Faith in him? Not likely. But he'd dumped Emma to do his duty by his family, and despite how it all went down, even she could see at the time that doing so had cost Konstantin. Not enough to maintain their relationship, but walking away hadn't been easy.

"If I learned one thing about you, it is how committed you are to your family, Konstantin. While I have *no* faith in you, I do have faith in that. Now you've acknowledged Mickey is yours, you won't try to shuttle him out of your life."

He opened his mouth to say something, but she forestalled him with a raised hand. "Even if you tried, I wouldn't let you. I will never let you hurt my son again."

"*Our* son. And I have no intention of hurting him. Or you."

"Leave me out of it."

"You are his mother—you are in the center of *it*."

Princesses by Royal Decree

Their place at the royal altar awaits...

The time has come for royal brothers King Nikolai and Princes Konstantin and Dimitri of Mirrus to wed. Their journeys to the altar will be just as they rule—by royal decree!

Lady Nataliya was contracted to marry a prince from Mirrus but is shocked when King Nikolai, whom she's secretly desired for years, steps in instead!

Emma's affair with Prince Konstantin is forced to end when his duty calls, but she's carrying a secret that will bind them forever!

Jenna's a fashion journalist and has no desire to be a princess, but her interest in Prince Dimitri could change everything...

Read Nataliya and Nikolai's story in
Queen by Royal Appointment

Discover Emma and Konstantin's story in
His Majesty's Hidden Heir

Both available now!

Look out for Jenna and Dimitri's story,
coming soon!

Lucy Monroe

HIS MAJESTY'S
HIDDEN HEIR

HARLEQUIN
PRESENTS

Recycling programs
for this product may
not exist in your area.

ISBN-13: 978-1-335-56810-6

His Majesty's Hidden Heir

Copyright © 2021 by Lucy Monroe

This edition published by arrangement with Harlequin Books S.A.

For questions and comments about the quality of this book,
please contact us at CustomerService@Harlequin.com.

Harlequin Enterprises ULC
22 Adelaide St. West, 40th Floor
Toronto, Ontario M5H 4E3, Canada
www.Harlequin.com

Printed in U.S.A.

USA TODAY bestselling author **Lucy Monroe** lives and writes in the gorgeous Pacific Northwest. While she loves her home, she delights in experiencing different cultures and places on her travels, which she happily shares with her readers through her books. A lifelong devotee of the romance genre, Lucy can't imagine a more fulfilling career than writing the stories in her head for her readers to enjoy.

Books by Lucy Monroe

Harlequin Presents

Million Dollar Christmas Proposal
Kostas's Convenient Bride
The Spaniard's Pleasurable Vengeance
After the Billionaire's Wedding Vows...

Ruthless Russians

An Heiress for His Empire
A Virgin for His Prize

Princesses by Royal Decree

Queen by Royal Appointment

Visit the Author Profile page
at Harlequin.com for more titles.

For my new editor, Carly Byrne. This is the first book we worked on together and I enjoyed it immensely. I'm looking forward to your insights on many more.

CHAPTER ONE

EMMA WALKED INTO her bank in downtown Santa Fe, her son's hand clasped tightly in her own.

There had been a tech glitch with the automatic deposits on payroll this month and the company had been forced to cut paper checks for all their employees. She hoped it was an anomaly.

Errands like this with an active four-nearly-five-year-old were not her favorite thing. Besides, since she was now working full-time as a bookkeeper, Emma preferred her time with Mickey to be focused on things that her son enjoyed.

He'd gotten used to having her around as she'd worked as a childminder to put herself through college, taking online courses part-time. She'd kept him with her since birth. The past year had been an adjustment for both of them since she'd finally gotten her degree and landed a job with decent pay and benefits.

Waiting in line at the bank, where he had to be quiet and stay still, was not her son's idea of fun. He liked to be moving, not still and quiet.

"Mom, how long?" he demanded, the spitting image of his father, his tone and manner only adding to the similarity.

Sometimes, Emma found it jarring how alike Mickey was to his biological father, though her son had never met the man. Anyone who knew the Prince would see His Royal Highness in his son within seconds of meeting Mickey.

Emma smiled down at her son. "Just a little while longer. See? There are only three people ahead of us."

"Then we can go for shaved ice?" Her son loved his shaved ice, but always managed to cover himself in sticky syrup by the time he'd finished even a small cup.

Inwardly sighing at the mess to come, Emma nodded nevertheless.

"Yes!"

She laughed. "Indoor voice, all right?"

"Okay, Mom." Could her son's tone be any more long-suffering?

A disturbance near the back of the bank drew her attention and Emma looked up. A group of businessmen in polished suits were exiting into the large lobby of the downtown branch, the aura of power around them a palpable thing.

One of the security guards that discreetly accompanied the group seemed familiar to Emma. He turned his head and she recognized him only a second before her eyes collided with the decadent chocolate brown gaze of the man she'd been sure she would never see again.

Prince Konstantin of Mirrus.

Second son to the small country's former King and the man who had not only broken her heart, but abandoned their son.

His eyes widened in instant recognition.

Memories of the last time they saw each other assaulted Emma like a bad movie she couldn't look away from.

They'd both been at university when they first met. He'd been twenty-three, in his last year of getting his MBA. She'd been nineteen, in her first year of business school. They'd run into each other in the quad.

It had been such a cliché. She'd dropped some books; he'd picked them up.

Their eyes had met and she'd felt like she'd been hit by a train. She hadn't known he was a prince, or that the men standing at a discreet distance were not other students, but his security detail.

He'd smiled, white teeth flashing below gorgeous brown eyes. Nearly six and a half feet tall, he'd towered over Emma's respectable five feet seven inches. Muscular and handsome, he'd taken her breath away. And her ability to speak.

He hadn't been put off by Emma's inability to voice her thanks. Rather, he'd seemed charmed by it.

"I believe these are yours." He'd held out her books.

She'd taken them with a silent nod.

"New to campus?"

They were nearing the end of the first semester of the year, but she'd nodded anyway.

"Would you like to go out with me?"

She'd managed a word then. "Yes."

While that memory was bittersweet, it was the ones that came later that caused so much pain in Emma's chest.

They'd dated for nearly a year, moving in together against her parents' wishes the summer after her freshman year. Despite his having told her at the start that he'd signed some kind of medieval contract to eventually marry the niece of another country's king, Kon had acted like he couldn't live without her.

He'd been attentive and caring, always charming, and incredibly passionate.

Emma had built dreams of the future around his behavior, rather than his words.

Then the ax had fallen.

"What did you just say?" Emma couldn't take in the words.

Kon *couldn't* mean them.

"My father wants me to honor the contract now. We have to break up. You're going to need to find somewhere else to live."

"No. You don't mean that."

Kon looked pained. "Emma, you knew this was coming."

"No." She shook her head, screaming inside from the pain. "No. You want to make love every day. You want to talk to me all the time when you're gone. You don't want to marry someone else."

He couldn't.

She'd thought, when he'd asked her to move in with him, that the contract was a nonissue. He'd never brought it up again. Emma had simply forced herself to ignore its existence, choosing to focus on the here and now. She loved Kon, and while he'd never used those words with her, his actions made her believe she was just as necessary to him as he was to her.

"It is not a matter of wanting to marry her. I made a promise. I must keep it."

"What? No, you signed that contract five years ago. You were just a kid."

"I hope not. You were the same age when we started dating."

She was twenty now, but not a lot wiser apparently. And he was twenty-four, also not a lot wiser if he was going to marry a woman he did not love for the sake of his family's consequence and business.

The argument had devolved from there. Emma had cried, and she wasn't proud remembering she'd begged him to reconsider. But Kon? He'd taken on his Prince Konstantin mantle, remaining aloof and cold, refusing to engage.

He'd offered her a year living in the apartment rent-free as a transition.

It had felt like a payoff and it was in that moment she'd known they were truly over.

Emma's heart had disintegrated in an explosion of pain. She'd moved out that night, going home to her parents with her tail tucked between her legs.

That hadn't worked out either, but those memories weren't going to take hold now.

She wouldn't let them.

Emma forced herself to stop playing the memory reel in her head and to focus on the present. The feel of her son's hand in hers. The sounds of the other bank customers and tellers speaking. Paper shuffling. Pens scratching as people signed things.

Knowing what was coming next, Emma should look away first. For her pride's sake. No way would His Royal Highness want to acknowledge he knew her.

She never considered he might not recognize her.

Even her ex-lover wasn't that oblivious.

She couldn't make herself look away though. Even after more than five years, her heart beat a mad rhythm at the sight of him and her eyes soaked him in like water to a thirsty plant.

But she was not thirsty. Not for him.

She had gotten over Konstantin. Had learned to hate him, in fact. And then learned to let that hatred go. Emma had had no choice. She wasn't living her life with the thorns of bitterness piercing her soul on a daily basis.

She did yoga. She meditated. She did not hate.

But right that minute? Seeing him so confident and unconcerned with his business cohorts, Emma was really having difficulty remembering patience, compassion and tolerance.

"Mom."

Her son's voice did what her own willpower had been unable to accomplish and broke her focus on the royal rat. Okay, tolerance wasn't going to be her strong suit today.

Emma looked down and found a strained smile for the little boy. "Yes, pumpkin?"

"I'm not a pumpkin." Her son's face, so like his father's, creased in a cranky frown. "I'm a boy."

Mickey was going through a phase of not liking endearments. He was not a pumpkin. Not sweet. Not darling. He barely tolerated the nickname Mickey over Mikhail, the name she'd had him christened. As he kept reminding her, he was a big boy. Almost five.

Heaven help her when he hit his teens.

"Yes, you are a wonderful little boy."

"I'm almost five!" he said loudly, clearly offended again. Being referred to as little was also on the banned list.

But she only grinned, despite the nervous tension

thrumming through her at that sighting of his sperm donor. "You are four…*and three-quarters*," she tacked on to appease. "And while you may be big for your age, you are still *my* little boy."

"And mine too, I think." Konstantin had crossed the vast lobby of the bank very quickly.

But why he had done so when *he* had taken out the restraining order that prevented her from getting within fifty feet of him, she had no idea. And then his words registered, and Emma wanted to hit him.

With her fist. Not her palm.

The unutterable rat!

Compassion was definitely out the window too.

Of course Mickey was his. She'd tried to tell Konstantin, but he'd kept her at a distance and his efforts to do so had made life for her and their son so much harder than it had to be.

She glared up at him. "Go away, Konstantin." Her mouth clamped shut. Calling him by name felt way too personal now.

But she didn't think referring to him as Prince Rat was going to go over well.

"I am going nowhere." He pointed down to Mickey, who was watching them both in rapt fascination, the recognition in his eyes impossible to miss. "That is my son and you have withheld him from me, for years."

Heat and cold washed over Emma in waves. She knew only one thing.

She was finally going to get her say, but she didn't want to have it here. Not with a bevy of rich executives and bank customers looking on.

"It's my daddy. That man is my daddy." Mickey

tugged urgently at Emma's hand, his voice carrying in the cavernous lobby.

Gasps could be heard and whispers, but Emma ignored them all, including the man staring at her as if the ceiling had just fallen on his head, to look down at her son. "Does he look like the pictures?"

Mickey slid eyes the same chocolate brown as his father's to the Prince and then back to meet his mother's gaze. "He doesn't look so mad in the pictures." His voice wobbled just a little, his usual confidence clearly shaken by Konstantin's attitude. "Doesn't he like me?"

"Of course I like you. You are my son." Konstantin's tone was nothing like filled with its usual arrogance. In fact, he sounded sick. "You've shown him pictures of me?" he asked her.

She didn't know if he was angry, relieved or entirely unimpacted by that fact.

Emma gave a short nod of agreement.

"But you did not tell me about him."

"Do we have to do this here?" she asked him, wishing they did not have to do *this* at all. She'd come to terms with the truth that her son would never meet his father until Mickey was of an age to contact the royal family of Mirrus on his own, DNA test results in hand.

This scene, right now, was out of some kind of horror novel. Her worst nightmare.

"We will go back to my hotel."

She shook her head. "No." She wasn't stupid. She knew this man had diplomatic status. She wasn't sure if that made his hotel room his own little fiefdom while he was in Santa Fe, but she wasn't taking any chances. "You can come to our home. In an hour. I need to finish running errands."

"You and my son are not leaving my sight."

"Then I guess you can follow us around as I finish the things I need to do," she said sarcastically.

"Do not be ridiculous. We need to talk."

"I need to deposit my check and then *I* need to buy groceries."

"My staff can take care of both."

"You think I'd trust your staff with *my* paycheck?" She would never let him hurt her, or more important, their son, again.

He jerked as if she'd hit him like she'd wanted to only moments before. "Why not?"

Emma did her best to give her son a natural smile. "Mickey, can you be a big boy and hold my place in line. I'm going to be right there." She pointed to a spot about ten feet away where she planned to set Konstantin straight out of her son's hearing.

"You'll both be right there?" her son asked.

Emma nodded.

"Okay, Mom. I'll stand right here." Mickey drew himself up importantly.

Emma said nothing to Konstantin before stepping away to the spot she'd indicated, her attention never leaving her son.

"Because I don't trust you at all," she whispered to Konstantin fiercely while smiling reassuringly at her son. "I don't trust you not to have the check tossed just to cause me further pain and embarrassment. I don't trust you not to use the information on it to find my employer and have me sacked. I don't—"

"I get the picture. You think I am some kind of monster."

"No, just a royal rat who has hurt me before in ways

I never would have expected and I'll never make the mistake of not *expecting* it ever again."

He turned and strode back to the group of men who had been with him, saying something to one of the men in the business suits. Suddenly, she was collecting Mickey and they were being led to a teller and getting her check deposited with all due haste.

"If you give a list to Sergei, he will see that your groceries are purchased."

One of the security men stepped forward with a nod.

She sighed. "Fine, but I've only budgeted seventy-five dollars and if he goes over buying the more expensive brands, I'm not paying for it. And all fresh veg, meat and dairy have to be organic." She frowned up at Sergei. "You can get those things most economically at—" Emma named one of the three stores she had to shop at to get the healthiest food for her son on the tightest budget.

"I will take care of it," Sergei promised.

"Give me your number and I'll send you my grocery list." She kept it in an app on her phone.

That taken care of, she led the way out of the bank and into the Santa Fe sunshine. "What are you doing in New Mexico?"

She had never once anticipated quite literally running into a prince in the place she'd chosen to start over for its lower cost of living and family-friendly environment.

"A mining deal." He said it like that should have been obvious.

"But—"

"You are aware that minerals are a strong natural resource in this state." It was a statement, not a question.

"I am now." She'd come to Santa Fe looking for a fresh start.

The only major industries that registered with her were ones she might work in. She'd settled in Santa Fe, rather than somewhere else in New Mexico, because of the numerous art galleries and thriving artist community.

She'd been supplementing her income with small commissions from one of them since a year after her move from Seattle. For a place to live and her main income, she'd watched children for a wealthy couple who had a real estate business. When Emma had gone job hunting, none of the places she'd applied to had been mining companies.

It had taken her nearly four years to build her life back to something decent, where she and her son did not have to live a hand-to-mouth existence and she wasn't going to let Konstantin mess it up now.

She'd gotten her degree, only an associate's and not the bachelor's she'd planned for, but it was a degree. But in order to get away from the stigma of the restraining order he'd taken out against her, Emma had had to change her name.

It had hurt to give up her adoptive parents' name. She'd been a Sloan since only a few months after birth.

However, they'd washed their hands of her, so she'd done it, changing both her and her son's last name to the one she'd been born with, Carmichael. The only thing she had of biological parents she would never know.

There was drama at the car, Mickey not wanting his father to leave and follow in another car, his screams and tears not unusual for his age, but having a more profound impact on Emma because of the situation. Moisture burned in the back of her own eyes as she tried to explain that Konstantin would meet them at their small house.

"I will ride with you," he said as he walked around the car to the passenger side.

She stared at him and then down at her ten-year-old domestic compact and tried to compute that statement. Him ride with her and Mickey?

Konstantin's security argued, but he ignored them, opening the back door for Mickey and helping her incredibly independent son, who had stopped allowing her to help him more than a year ago, into his safety seat.

Hands shaking with nerves, Emma spoke to Konstantin across the roof of the car. "You can ride with your security. Mickey will settle."

Her son was no longer crying because he believed Konstantin would be riding with them, but was now busy doing up the buckles on his five-point harness.

She acknowledged ruefully that he was no longer the one in danger of having a meltdown.

Konstantin closed Mickey's door, tapped the hood and came around the car to speak to her.

"You kept my son from me." The accusation in his voice would have hurt.

If the words had been true.

They were not.

A parking lot was better than a bank, but the car was not exactly soundproof. She lowered her voice, but let her tone drip with accusation. "You ejected me from your life so you could marry another woman."

"And so out of spite, you did this thing!" The Prince was making no effort to keep his voice down.

"Spite? Are you delusional?" she demanded, her voice still low. "I tried to call you. You refused my calls. I tried to see you, and you had a restraining order taken out against me, remember that? I'd done nothing to warrant one, but men like you, they get what they want."

"I am not the delusional one. I took out no restraining order. More to the point, I did not *want* to be a nonentity in my child's life," he said in a driven tone.

"You couldn't tell from how you treated me." He had made it clear he wanted to be a nonentity in *her* life and his dedication to that endeavor had dictated his not finding out about their son.

"You should have tried harder."

How typical to expect her to have had options he would have taken for granted, but that he'd removed from her. He lived in such a rarified world, he probably really believed the garbage he was spouting.

"What do you mean, harder? I called and texted, but you blocked my number. You moved out of our apartment and I couldn't get a forwarding address." She'd tried, but the building super and doormen had held firm against charm, pleading and even threats. "I wrote and you never answered, I didn't even know if you got my letters. I sent emails through the contact form on the Mirrus Global website, but never got a reply."

It had been hellish. And once she *had* finally gotten in touch with someone in his family? That hell had only gotten worse, not better.

Something like guilt briefly showed in his expression and then it was gone.

Konstantin looked down at their son through the window, realized the small boy was watching them avidly even if he couldn't hear everything said and grimaced. "We will have this discussion later."

"Good call." She made no effort to temper her sarcasm. But neither did she reopen the conversation.

Emma tried to protest his riding with them again when he walked around to the passenger door, but he shook his head. "I told him I would, so I will." Then the Prince climbed into her car and pulled his seat belt into place, like he rode in such humble transportation all the time.

Mickey kept up a running dialogue with his father as Emma drove, stopping every few sentences, to get her confirmation. "Right, Mom?" was one of his favorite phrases when he was feeling nervous.

The number of times he used that phrase in the short drive to their house on the outskirts of town indicated just how nervous he was feeling, despite the confident demeanor he put forth.

So much like his father, she ached. As she often did at that reminder.

When they arrived at the fixer-upper house she'd managed to buy only a month previously, Konstantin did not look impressed. She tried to see the one-level old adobe house through his eyes and failed utterly. She could see only what had drawn her to it first.

The coral-stained adobe contrasted happily with the wood trim painted turquoise. The landscaping needed work as odd scrub grew between and around the natural rock that acted as tile in the tiny front courtyard.

She did her best to keep up on the weeds, but she had only so many off-hours.

"Is this your home?" Konstantin asked.

Emma didn't know if he was talking to her or to their son, but Mickey answered. "We just got it. I have my own room now and Mom is gonna put in a play structure in back when we get enough money."

Konstantin made a sound like he was choking, but he smiled at Mickey. "I would like to see your room."

"Okay. That's okay, right, Mom?" Mickey asked again.

"Of course." She turned off the car. "Let's go inside."

Konstantin stopped once they were in the living room and just stared around him. "This is where you and *my* son live?" he asked with what sounded like disdain to her sensitive ears.

Emma gritted her teeth, gave their son a significant look and then replied, "Yes. This is the home *our* son loves and is very proud to be able to call his own. Think before you speak, Konstantin. I mean, Your Highness."

He frowned. "You used to call me Kon."

"We used to be friends." They'd been lovers too, but she wasn't saying that in front of her son.

"We are going to be much more than that soon. Call me Konstantin if you must, but don't use my title. We are way beyond that." With that pronouncement he headed down the hallway with Mickey.

The next two hours were a revelation. Konstantin should not have been so good with Mickey. He had no experience with children. He was a tycoon prince, not a dad.

But he was patient with the little boy, showing no frustration when Mickey grew fractious.

"It's time for lunch, I think." Emma smiled down at her son. "Are you hungry, Mickey?"

"My name is Mikhail!" her son shouted.

Emma winced at the volume, but her reaction was nothing compared with how still Konstantin became. "You named him after me? But why?"

She stepped back, though he'd made no move to come closer to her. She'd been very careful to keep her distance and their son between them. She had no answer she was willing to say in front of Mickey for why she'd given her son his father's middle name.

It hadn't been because she wanted to honor Konstantin, but she'd thought her son deserved something of his father's and that was all Emma had ever been able to give him.

She just shook her head. "Lunch."

"Because you're my dad," Mickey replied with none of his mother's reticence. "Mom says I'm just like you."

"Does she?" Konstantin stared at her and then at Mickey.

Mickey nodded. "Mostly when I'm being stubborn."

"Like about eating lunch?"

"I don't want you to go away."

Oh, man. Emma had never doubted that Mickey needed his dad, but she'd had no way to give him access. Now Prince Konstantin Mikhail of the House of Merikov was here in the flesh and Mickey didn't want to lose him.

Resolve firmed inside Emma. Whatever Konstantin had planned, he was going to play a significant part in his son's life from this point forward. Even if Emma had to go to the media and shame him into it.

Tiana, the former Queen of Mirrus and his sister-in-law, not to mention the woman who had threatened to take her baby away, was dead now. It was time for Emma to stop acting out of fear of Konstantin's family.

"I am going nowhere," Konstantin promised.

Emma only hoped he meant it.

"Would you like to eat lunch with us?" she invited.

See her remembering manners taught by her parents and patience taught by her yogi.

"Yes, thank you." Konstantin looked surprised by the offer. "What would you like? I will send Sergei out for it."

Sergei had been careful to stay close, but always shifting to a different room than the one she, Mickey and Konstantin were in. The rest of the detail were outside watching her front and back door for threats, but probably just as much for paparazzi sniffing around.

"Thank you for the offer, but Mickey needs to eat now, or he's going to get *hangry* and none of us wants to deal with that."

"Hangry? I am not familiar with this term."

"Hungry and angry together. *Hangry.*"

Konstantin smiled. "I too can become *hangry*," he admitted to Mickey. "We should both eat lunch."

"We'll all eat together at the table, like a family. That's okay, right, Mom?" Mickey's nerves were showing again.

"Yes. We'll all eat together. Do you want to help me make sandwiches?"

"Will Dad…" He looked at Konstantin as if asking if that was okay.

The Prince nodded at his son, swallowing like he was having trouble containing emotion.

"Will *Dad* help us make them too?" Mickey asked, stressing his father's title like he was savoring it.

Tears burned at the back of Emma's eyes and she hated Konstantin more in that moment than she ever had before. For all he'd stolen from Mickey, for the fear of loss her son couldn't hide.

Konstantin met her gaze and something must have shown on her face because he flinched backward as if she'd struck him.

Emma forced her anger deep inside, repeating the mantra she'd used to let go of her hatred in the first place and gave her son the reassuring smile he needed. "I'm not sure Konstantin has ever made a sandwich before. You can show him how to spread the mayo."

Emma insisted on making sandwiches for the security detail as well as the three of them, which she knew meant she'd have to dip into the rainy day fund to buy more groceries, but needs must. Konstantin tried to argue with her that his people didn't need to be fed by her, but she ignored him.

What did *he* know about what the average person needed? He lived in his rarified world and had no clue what it meant to be just a regular guy.

Cooking with her ex-lover in her tiny kitchen turned into a test of Emma's strength.

He kept brushing up against her and sending her senses into orbit. And the worst part? She didn't think he even realized he was doing it.

There just wasn't enough space *not* to bump into each other with three of them working at the counter, putting the food together. She pulled a container of gazpacho she'd made the day before out and dished it up to go with the sandwiches for everyone.

The day was warm and chilled soup would be refreshing. Never mind it was supposed to be her and Mickey's dinner two nights next week.

"You're gonna like this, Dad," Mickey assured Konstantin. "Mom's the best cook!"

"I remember a time when she struggled to boil water." He smiled at her, inviting her to share the joke.

Emma's mother had been old-fashioned in so many ways, but her kitchen was her private domain and she never allowed anyone in it. Not even her daughter. Emma had had no clue how to cook when she'd gone to college.

"I learned." When she'd been pregnant and alone.

Konstantin frowned, like her thoughts were broadcast for him to see. Maybe they were. Emma had never had much of a poker face. Her dad used to tease her that he knew if she liked her presents, not by what she said when she opened them, but by what her face told him.

Some days, she missed her parents so much, it hurt.

But like Konstantin, they'd opted to eject Emma from their lives when she wasn't what they wanted her to be.

"You look sad. What is wrong?"

He was asking her that? Like he couldn't guess, if not the particulars, then certainly the gist. And what gave him the right to ask any personal questions of her at all anyway?

She inhaled and exhaled repeating *patience*, *compassion* and *tolerance* under her breath.

"Mom gets like that," Mickey said practically. "She

says memories aren't always warm and happy, but they're still ours. It's okay if I cry sometimes when I remember Snoopy dying."

"Who is Snoopy?"

"He was the family dog for the people I worked for."

"Worked?" he asked, probing.

But she ignored him and started handing out plates.

"You are not their servant. They can come get their food if you insist on feeding them."

"Don't you think they deserve to eat?" she asked with bite.

He frowned at her, seemingly shocked. "You know me better than that. They could have gotten takeout. I would have paid for it."

"Instead, I chose to feed them."

"I don't remember you being this stubborn."

"Life changes us all."

Lunch was a surprisingly convivial meal, but by the end of it, Mickey was practically drooping off his chair. "Nap time for you."

"I will be here when you wake," Konstantin promised, staving off what might have been another meltdown.

Her son was tired. He was stressed. And he was terrified he'd never again see this person he'd just gotten to call *Dad*.

Mickey insisted on holding Konstantin's hand on the way to his bedroom.

"Bathroom first," Emma insisted from behind them.

Mickey didn't argue, just veered into the brightly tiled, if small room. She'd taken pains to get the grout clean, but she didn't have the knowhow to fix the chips in the mosaic tiles put in when the house had been built more than forty years ago, or the money to hire someone to do it.

Emma tucked her son in, but he extracted no fewer than three more promises from Konstantin that he would be there when Mickey woke up.

She just hoped the Prince realized how important it was that he keep that promise.

CHAPTER TWO

TYPICALLY, THOUGH THEY were in her home, Konstantin led the way as they left Mickey's room.

He went unerringly into the living room. Granted the house was small, so it wasn't likely he'd get lost looking for the main rooms.

Konstantin sat on the yellow sofa and she settled into the chair covered in a complementary print of Aztec shapes. The Prince looked around the room, his intelligent gaze taking in every detail.

It wasn't high-end decor, but it wasn't shabby. Emma had decorated with Southwestern designs and bright colors, throwing rugs over the wooden floors that needed refinishing.

She was proud of what she'd managed to accomplish for her and her son. "Not what you're used to?"

"I can see you here. Your love of color and interesting shapes. It's everywhere. You've really bought into the whole Southwestern motif, haven't you?"

Was he referring to the house, or the way she was dressed in a striped poncho-style shirt, denim capris and sandals with conches on the top? Probably both.

"This is my home now." She'd found a sense of belonging and acceptance in *The City Different.*

"So, you have gone native?" he teased.

She shrugged. "I think we have more important things to talk about than my sense of style."

He sighed, and then nodded, looking pained. "I gave instructions."

"Instructions?"

"Before. After we broke up."

"What sort of instructions?" As if she didn't know, but he could spell it out.

"I told my PAA to block all attempts at contact."

Well, that explained the lack of response to her emails, messages left on his work voice mail and letters sent to his office. It did not explain his ignoring the letters she'd sent to the palace in Mirrus or her attempts to contact him via his role as Prince.

Then again, she wouldn't have been on the approved contacts list and in that case it was unlikely he'd even had to *give instructions* to palace staff.

"I wonder if I had written about the pregnancy instead of leaving numerous messages asking you to call me, if your PAA would have ignored those instructions."

"I told her not to read anything from you, that there was *nothing* you had to say that I wanted to hear." And clearly he did not like admitting this.

Every strained line of his gorgeous face and his supertense posture testified to that fact.

"So, whose fault exactly is it that Mickey has gone nearly five years without meeting his father?" she asked, insisting Konstantin admit his culpability.

He had broken up with her and broken her heart. Fine. But he'd also abandoned their son and that would *never* be fine with her.

And maybe she wouldn't need him to admit his guilt if he hadn't kept harping on how *she* should have tried harder.

"You should have tried harder."

Was he kidding? Fury began to bubble up inside Emma and her best attempts at releasing it were not working. This man!

"I really can't believe you! You are such a product of your privilege," she indicted with exasperation. "Are you telling me you would have welcomed a media storm, naming you the father of my illegitimate child, *Your Highness*? Because that was the only option left open to me."

His expression left no doubt how little he liked that idea. "You could have gone to someone in my family and told them."

"You think I had the resources to fly to Mirrus and try to get an audience with royalty?" This man was not for real.

"You could have sold some jewelry."

"Trust me, I've sold every stinking, meaningless present you ever gave me so I could do my best by my son. But what about the way things went down over five years ago would have given me any belief that wasting precious financial resources trying to talk to *your family* would have made any difference?"

"I realize now that I should have left you an opening to contact me, but if you had just contacted the palace, insisted of speaking to one of my family… They would have listened and gotten a message to me."

Could he even hear himself? "You think if *I* called the palace and *insisted* on speaking to one of the royal family, I'd just be put through? What planet do you live on? Anyway, that just goes to show how much you know. I *did* email your sister-in-law."

Queen Tiana had been the only one Emma could find contact information for.

Of course, it had been an email associated with her position at a children's charity, so the initial email had been circumspect. And talking to that selfish whack job had been a huge mistake that only made Emma's precarious situation feel even more so.

"You put news of your pregnancy in an email to Tiana?" he demanded, sounding shocked and upset.

"Now you're showing your true colors," Emma derided. "You would have been furious if I'd gone to the press five and a half years ago. And no, I told her I needed to speak privately to her. I begged her to call me."

"But she did not."

"Worse." So much worse. "She did. And I told her I was pregnant."

"No."

"Yes."

"Then she did not believe the child was mine. My sister-in-law would have contacted me otherwise. We were friends."

"You were friends with that vicious harpy?"

"What the hell are you talking about?" Konstantin sounded so shocked, it would have been amusing if Emma wasn't so angry. "Tiana was neither vicious, nor a harpy."

Emma knew better. "Ever get into an argument with her?"

"She argued with you about the child being mine? I find that hard to believe. She knew we'd dated. She was the only person in my family that did."

"You chose *her* as your confidante?" Emma asked, appalled.

"I do not know why you are talking about her like this. She died and we all grieved her loss."

"Funny, but if she *weren't* dead, I would have a run a mile when I saw you in the bank. So, think on that."

"What did she say to you to cause such antipathy?"

"Besides her offer to *buy* my baby and my silence? Besides threaten me if I refused? Besides inform me with a very menacing demeanor that she was a queen and I was a nobody and she would get her way? Oh, really, nothing much."

"That's ridiculous. Tiana would never have done those things."

"She told me you would never believe the child was yours. That her way was the best way to make sure my baby was raised in the royal environment it deserved, only I thought he deserved a mother who loved him." Emotion choked Emma and she did her best to push it away.

She couldn't afford to let her own pain, remembered fear or even present anger take over during this conversation. Too much was at stake.

And while she wasn't a naive twenty-year-old any longer, she still didn't have the resources to fight a monarchy if he chose to go as crazy as his dead sister-in-law had.

"Surely you knew you had the trump card. You carried my DNA within your body."

"And I had the resources to force you to take a DNA test? Never mind how you could have paid someone off to give false results."

"I would never have done something so underhand." There he went sounding shocked again.

"Says the man who made it nearly impossible for me to get a decent job for the entire three years that restraining order based on *false* testimony was in place."

"I told you before, I took out no restraining order."

Something inside Emma just cracked open and all the anger she had been tamping down came surging up. She jumped up from her chair and pointed wrathfully at him. "You just stay there. I will be right back."

"No restraining order," she muttered to herself as she stomped down the hall. "He thinks he's going to gaslight me? Make me forget the hell he put me through? I've got the restraining order. I've got evidence. I'm not the crazy one here."

She spun the lock on the safe she kept copies of important papers in. Most had corresponding originals in her safe-deposit box at the bank. Call her paranoid, but after her trust had been betrayed by him, by her parents, by his crazy if dead sister-in-law, Emma was prepared for every eventuality she could be.

She stomped back into the living room and threw the court papers at him. "No restraining order? Then what is that? A bedtime story?"

"You're going to wake Mikhail if you keep shouting like that."

"Then he can see for himself what a rat he has for a father." Emma stomped to her chair and plopped into it, glaring at Konstantin as he read the document he held.

Her fury did not abate as horror came over his features. It did not diminish as he looked up from the papers, his face waxen and pale, his expression on the verge of being ill.

She didn't know what all that shock and horror was about.

"Didn't you think I'd keep a copy? It will read well in any attempt you make to get custody of Mickey. I can prove the accusations of stalking made in there are false. I won't be the one sporting the criminal record this time!"

"A restraining order is not a criminal record." The words came out low and shocked.

Emma made a dismissive gesture with her hand. Semantics! "Tell that to the employers that ran routine background checks on me and it popped up. Do you know how impossible it made trying to provide for myself and later for Mickey?"

Konstantin went from pale to sickly green. "I did not do this. I did not take out that order of restraint. I never would have."

"And yet, you did."

"I did not. Look at the papers."

"Oh, I know… The palace lawyers did it. Some guy named Albert Popov, but it was on your behalf. And it was issued on the weight of your testimony." No further proof required.

But then he was a prince. And she was a nobody.

He'd claimed she'd *stalked* him, said she'd had delusions of a relationship that never existed, had told the court that she had threatened him that if she could not have him, no one could. Only his fabrications hadn't been well researched. He'd had to put dates and times with the claims, and Emma had proof she was with other people, in class and one time even at a doctor's appointment when she was supposed to have accosted him.

She had signed affidavits to that effect in her safety deposit too.

At one time, she'd considered forcing the issue, but she'd realized that doing so had to be a last resort. Because even with the proof the TRO had been gotten under false pretenses, she was still one person and he represented a monarchy.

She felt stronger now, more centered and capable of fighting than she had at age twenty.

"No. I never said any of those things," he said now, sounding so darn sincere.

She wanted to smack him and that thought made her feel guilty. Patience, compassion and tolerance, she reminded herself.

Without a lot of effect.

"Rewriting history now, *Your Highness*?" she sneered.

Allowing her anger to come out felt cleansing, good. Like a weight that wasn't hers to carry was being released. But she didn't feel any better about the past for voicing her pain to the man who had never cared that he'd hurt her in the first place.

"My son is nearly five and I have met him for the first time today. And it is my fault. That is what you are saying."

"Yes." She had no give in her for this man anymore. He'd done too much to hurt her, but even more damning, by his own actions he had also done a lot to make her son's life harder.

"You have grown very hard."

"I just opened my eyes to who you are."

"And it is not anyone good in your estimation."

She shrugged. "I wouldn't be open to your having a relationship with my son if I did not think there was any good in you." She just now knew how ruthless he could be. Knew that *she* could not trust him, even if Mickey might be able to.

She would never forget that truth again.

"He is my son too."

"Not so you would notice."

Konstantin winced. "What have you told him about me?"

"He only asked about his father when he started preschool. Other children had daddies, but he did not."

"And?"

"And I showed him pictures, told him that he would meet you someday when he was older."

"You told him this? So, you had some faith in me, then?"

"Not so much, no. But he's your spitting image and I didn't think once you met him, even a coldhearted bastard like you could deny his existence." Though the quickness with which Konstantin had latched onto Mickey being his was a small point in the rat's favor.

It had clearly never occurred to him that she might have jumped from his bed into that of another man.

"How was this meeting supposed to happen?" Konstantin asked, still subdued.

"Not the way it did, that's for sure."

"But you planned to try again. To tell me about him?"

"He deserved for me to."

"But I did not."

"Frankly, your feelings did not come into it for me."

"You have changed."

"So you've said."

"Five and a half years ago, you lived for me."

"Five and a half years ago, if I hadn't been pregnant, I might well have died for you."

"Do not make melodramatic statements like that, even if you are merely trying to make a point." But he sounded shaken rather than condemning.

Which is why she maintained an even tone when she asked, "Melodrama?" She shook her head and that's when she told him about the mugging. It had happened the same night her parents had kicked her out.

She'd been mugged for the twenty-nine dollars she carried in her wallet. Emma hadn't had credit cards then. Her parents didn't believe in them. She'd just been taking a walk to clear her head, but the motel she'd landed in wasn't in the best part of the city.

"When I woke up in pain unlike any I'd ever known and remembered I literally had no place to go, no one to call to come help me, I had a moment when I just wanted to go back to sleep and never wake up. The doctor came in and told me that it would be touch-and-go for a while. For both of us. But that my baby was still alive inside me and I clung to that. I have never felt anything like my determination to give Mickey life. It *was* touch-and-go for almost a week, for both of us. But every time I surfaced to consciousness, I thought of my baby and determined to live."

Konstantin was gray. "Where were your parents?"

"Like you, they had decided that I was no longer suitable for the role I had in their life."

"They disowned you?" he asked in shock.

"Yes."

"And you probably blame me for this as well."

"No."

"Why not?"

"They adopted me, believing they could raise me to be a good, religious daughter. They tried their best, but I had sex with you outside the bounds of marriage and that was not acceptable. According to them, bad blood outed."

"Because you were pregnant and that was my fault."

"No, the choice to share my body with you? That was mine to make. And I made it. I took responsibility for it then and have done ever since."

"I seduced a virgin into my bed and kept her there as my mistress," he said with blatant self-condemnation.

But she'd never let anyone else take the blame for her choices. It wasn't in Emma to pass the buck like that. "I wanted to be seduced. The mistress part I could have done without, but if I wanted to share even a part of your life, I knew I had to be available to you when you had time for me and that meant allowing you to support me. Again, a decision I made."

A decision her parents had hated. Her coming up pregnant after moving home when he'd dumped her had been the final straw as far as Ansel and Belinda Sloan were concerned.

If Emma had been willing to give Mickey up, things might have been different, but she hadn't been. Not then. Not now.

Her son was her life and Prince Konstantin of Mirrus had better realize that.

"You did not decide to get pregnant."

"No. Even now I cannot credit that my IUD fell out without me being aware." What were the chances?

According to her OB, very slim, but not nonexistent. Obviously. Emma had just been unlucky. Though it was impossible to think of Mickey as anything but a gift in her life. The unplanned nature of her pregnancy was something else.

Emma shook off her thoughts. "My OB said it happens, not often, but it happens. I was just so happy the pain had stopped, I didn't question the whys."

"You never told me the IUD hurt."

"What part of the repressed, raised-to-ultraconservative-values me would have talked to you back then about something so private and embarrassing?"

"Sex is private and we talked about that."

She rolled her eyes. "Saying I want you is not the same thing as saying the lower half of my body feels like someone kicked it because of my IUD."

"It was that bad?"

"Yes."

"No wonder you did not want sex sometimes."

"No wonder."

"I thought you were losing interest in me."

"I guess that made you feel better about knowing you were going to dump me so you could marry another woman."

His expression said it all. Konstantin's belief she was losing interest *had* alleviated his guilt over making plans to marry Lady Nataliya.

That the woman had ended up married to his brother and *not* Konstantin was entirely beside the point.

"Five and a half years ago, that would have surprised me. I thought you were this amazing guy."

"But now you know differently." His tone was strange.

"You turned your ruthlessness on me when you excised me from your life. I've lived with the consequences of your selfishness every day since."

"You consider our son a consequence."

"I consider how hard it has been to provide for him with that stupid restraining order on my record a consequence. I consider how he has gone without any extended family since birth a consequence. I consider how he cried when he came home from school after they made gifts for their fathers a week after the ones done for Mother's Day, keeping it even, you see. Only for a little boy without a dad just the first of many times he would be faced with the knowledge he did not have a father."

"There are many single-parent households out there."

"Yes, and children with two parents of the same sex. Schools should be more sensitive, but his was not and my son cried because he lacked."

"And that was my fault."

"Yes."

"You don't think much of me."

"No."

"I am surprised you are open to me seeing Mikhail."

"Whatever is best for my son, if I can give it to him, I will."

"You could have married and given him a stepfather."

"Because being raised by parents who had not given birth to me worked out so well." She'd thought her adopted parents loved her. Emma had learned differently, and she wasn't letting anyone do that to her son.

"A parent can be neglectful or abusive, or anything

in between and have the strongest of blood ties with their child."

"Yes, but I wasn't going to risk bringing someone into Mickey's life that might not love him like I do."

"You are risking that with me."

"As much as it is not fair, and I cannot guarantee you will always be good for my son, you have had a place in his life since the day I conceived. You are his biological father and if you want to be his dad, for his sake, I have to let you try."

"You do not believe I will disappear from his life again, or you would not risk it regardless." He sounded very certain of that.

And he was right. "No, I don't."

"Even if I have more children at some later date?"

"Even then." Though something deep inside her recoiled at the thought of him having children with another woman.

"So, you at least have some faith in me."

Faith in him? Not likely. But he'd dumped her to do his duty by his family and despite how it all went down, even she could see at the time that doing so had cost Konstantin. Not enough to maintain their relationship, but walking away hadn't been easy.

At least she'd thought it hadn't. How efficiently he'd cut her out of her life and left no loophole for getting back in, even just to have a conversation so she could tell him she was pregnant?

That might tell a different story.

Regardless, she did know one thing about him. "If I learned one thing about you, it is how committed you are to your family, Konstantin. While I have *no* faith in you, I do have faith in that. Now you've acknowl-

edged Mickey is yours, you won't try to shuttle him
out of your life."

He opened his mouth to say something, but she forestalled him with a raised hand. "Even if you tried,
I wouldn't let you. I will never let you hurt my son
again."

"*Our* son and I have no intention of hurting him.
Or you."

"Leave me out of it."

"You are his mother—you are in the center of *it*."

Emma stood. "I paint during Mickey's nap time. If
you'll excuse me." She wasn't hanging out with Konstantin chatting about old times.

Emma had had her say.

In her opinion, the Prince needed time to digest the
home truths she'd served up.

Not that he took it.

She could hear Konstantin on the phone and then
instructing someone to bring him his laptop. Working. Typical.

He'd just found out he had a son, but Mirrus Global
still came first.

It would do Emma well to remember the Prince's
priorities.

She took some time to center herself and get her
feelings back under control before she picked up her
paints and went to work on her latest commission.

CHAPTER THREE

"So, you are a painter?" Konstantin asked Emma when he tracked her down to a glassed-in porch that overlooked the back courtyard, which she'd clearly turned into her studio. She'd always wanted to pursue her art. "Good for you."

She had a paint-splattered apron over her clothes, her shoes were kicked in a corner and the image she presented reminded him so much of old times, he sucked in a breath as emotions he did not *do* assailed him.

Emma looked up, her expression unfocused and a little startled, like she'd forgotten she had a visitor. A far cry from the days when she hung on his every word. He missed the way she used to look at him because he was pretty sure he still looked at her like she was the most desirable woman walking the planet.

"Painting small commissions is a way I supplement my regular income."

Her parents had refused her an education at a fine arts college, insisting she get a more practical degree. When they'd been together, she'd been working on a BA in business.

He looked at the canvas on the easel. It was a paint-

ing of downtown Santa Fe. "That is very nice, but not
the art I remember you doing."

Five years ago her art had been splashy, vibrant colors filled with emotion.

She shrugged. "It pays the bills and I still get to put
my stamp on the artwork."

"I see art still has the same effect on your attitude.
You seem much calmer."

"Art and meditation. I spent the first ten minutes
in here meditating." She said it with no apology. No
embarrassment.

This woman no longer struggled with marching to her
own drum. When they'd been together, she'd hated dis-
appointing her parents, or being singled out as different.

"You meditate?" he asked. Fascinated.

"At least twice a day, more if Mickey is even more
active than usual. I do yoga too. Trust me, single parenting takes every ounce of patience and calm I have
and then some. So, I augment."

"In pretty unique ways."

"Not around here. Santa Fe is very proud of its *be
different* vibe."

"Mirrus isn't exactly backward, but I don't know if
we even have a yoga studio."

"You probably do, but since you don't use it, you
wouldn't know."

"You're saying I'm oblivious."

She shrugged. "You will take my words the way
you want."

"You sound very Zen."

"Mickey is going to wake soon. He'll be glad you
kept your promise."

"Did you think I wouldn't?"

"I didn't think about it. Worrying wouldn't change your actions, only my anxiety levels." And she smiled.

Art and meditation. A winning combination for Emma's peace of mind. He would remember that, make it easy for her to do both whenever she felt the need.

And that smile? Went straight to his groin. Not the reaction she was looking for with her sound bites of wisdom, he was sure.

"I've been looking for you for the past several months." He'd been on the verge of hiring a private investigator, or swallowing his pride and asking his new sister-in-law for help.

"Why?"

"I'm sure you know Lady Nataliya is now the Princess of Mirrus. I think my brother is going to make her Queen on their anniversary." Which wasn't the real answer to Emma's question.

That was way more complicated.

Over five years ago, he'd been committed to following through with the marriage contract, but breaking up with Emma had been much harder than he'd expected. He'd needed time to grieve the loss of their relationship, even though he hadn't acknowledged that was what he was doing.

He'd dreamed about her nightly and then less frequently as time went on, but the dreams never stopped completely. He'd never stopped seeing Emma in other women only to realize it wasn't her.

She had *haunted* him.

And so Konstantin had put off marrying a woman he'd been pretty sure had a thing for his brother. As much as he'd wanted to please his father, he'd been unable to take those final steps to court Nataliya and announce a formal engagement.

Then Tiana had died, and the family had gone into formal mourning. The question of Konstantin getting married anytime soon became a moot point, not to be raised by anyone, but certainly not him, for another five years.

It shouldn't have surprised him, considering the role she'd played in him putting off his marriage to Nataliya to begin with, that once his commitment to Nataliya was out of the way, Konstantin hadn't been able to stop wondering about Emma.

What was she doing? Was she still single?

"You say Mirrus isn't backward, but seriously?" Emma was asking now. "Your brother has to *make* his wife queen, or he can keep her as a princess for their whole marriage? Talk about being under the thumb of the patriarchy."

"It's a political role, not just a title. You cannot blame my brother for being cautious." Why were they talking about Nikolai and Nataliya?

That's your fault, genius, his inner voice reminded him.

"The fact the law is written the way it is feeds the power of patriarchy."

"You've become very political."

"You think having an opinion about equal rights and opportunities for women makes me political?" she asked.

Put that way? Maybe not. "But the issues *are* politicized."

"Issues become politicized when you have one

group trying to suppress another. That doesn't inherently make the issues themselves political."

"That's an interesting take."

"Isn't it?"

"Dad, you're still here!"

Konstantin spun around at the sound of his son's voice. Mikhail was still rubbing sleep from his eyes, his little-boy features so familiar it stalled Konstantin's breath for a second. He managed a nod.

Mikhail looked at his mother. "He's still here, Mom."

"Yes, he is, Mickey."

"When is he going away again?" Mickey asked.

Before she could answer, Konstantin found his voice. "I am not going away. Now that I have found you and your mom, I will never lose you again."

"You lost us?"

Konstantin looked to Emma. He didn't want to contradict anything she had told their son.

Emma's eyes glistened, but her features showed that newfound serenity she'd managed to achieve since coming in here. "He did."

"You didn't know he was looking for us?" Mikhail asked his mother.

She shook her head. "No. I thought he did not have a place in his life for us."

"Oh. But he does?"

"I do," Konstantin affirmed.

"Mom said you are a prince, but you know… Princes are only in fairy tales." Mikhail cast a sidelong glance at his mother, but he didn't seem worried she'd be upset he was checking on her veracity.

"Do you like fairy tales?" Konstantin asked him.

"Not really. I like…" Mikhail named a popular children's series about an animal family. "There's a mom and dad and grandparents and everything."

"You have a grandfather, two uncles and aunt who will be delighted to meet you. One of your uncles *is* a king, but we aren't a fairy tale."

"Really? Am I a prince?"

"No, but you are an earl." Though not officially. Not yet. But Konstantin would make sure Mikhail had his rightful place in the family as his eldest child.

"What's an earl?"

"It is a title of nobility. It means you are a member of the Royal Family of Mirrus."

Mikhail's nose and forehead scrunched in thought. "But my mom is not a princess."

"No." Not yet.

"That's good."

"It is?"

"Yeah. She gets real messy with her paints sometimes and when she gardens. And when she did the floors in my room? She got sweaty, like whoa."

Konstantin couldn't hold back a smile at his son's reply and phrasing. He looked at Emma, sharing the joke. "Like whoa?"

"He picked it up at his preschool day care."

"My teacher says it," Mikhail informed them, his tone revealing the boy's admiration for the teacher.

Emma's smile for their son was loving and a little amused. "Yes, he does."

"You don't think princesses get messy or sweaty?" Konstantin asked Mikhail.

"Do they?" Mikhail asked rather than answered, his face alight with little-boy curiosity.

"They do."

Mikhail gave Emma a dubious look. "I guess you can be a princess, Mom."

Emma laughed, the sound filled with genuine amusement. "That's all right, sweetie. I'll stick with plain old Emma Carmichael."

Not if Konstantin had anything to say about it.

Konstantin paced his hotel room while he spoke in rapid Russian to his brother King Nikolai of Mirrus.

"Yes, she had a copy of the restraining order," he said to his brother Nikolai now.

"But why would Sir Popov take it on himself to take out a TRO on your behalf? Did you say it is based on testimony given by you?" Nikolai demanded, sounding as judgmental as only an older brother who was also a king and had never done anything stupid like break up with the mother of his child could.

Needing to understand where the TRO had come from, Konstantin had called the senior palace lawyer, Sir Albert Popov, Esquire, before reaching out to Nikolai.

The phone call had been as confusing as it had been illuminating.

Konstantin was trying to figure out *why* Tiana had done what she had, even while he talked to his brother.

Popov had confirmed that the former Queen had been the one who had instructed him to take out the restraining order, based on trumped-up testimony supposedly supplied by *him*. After extracting further disturbing details from the palace lawyer, Konstantin had instructed the man to arrange an immediate flight to New Mexico.

Konstantin felt betrayed and furious and a lot of

other negative emotions he was doing his best to keep a lid on. He had to keep his head for both this discussion with his brother and to figure out where to go from here with Emma.

"Supposed testimony," Konstantin reminded his brother. "I would never lie about Emma that way." His brother should know that about him.

"Are you sure?"

"What the hell? Nikolai, I know you and I don't agree on everything but you know me better than that."

A sigh came over the phone. "You are right. I do. Sometimes…" His brother let his words trail off in very uncharacteristic fashion.

"What?"

"Sometimes, I get jealous and it makes me look at you differently."

"Jealous of what?"

"You were practically engaged to Nataliya."

Was his brother serious right now? "Are you kidding me? She's only ever had eyes for you, and I knew it. Why do you think I dragged my feet so hard on going through with the marriage?"

Who wanted to be married to a woman who would probably fantasize he was his brother on their wedding night?

"You weren't ready to get married."

"When we first signed that contract, she was eighteen, I was only a year older. Of course I wasn't ready to marry her then. But five and a half years ago, I broke things off with Emma so I could marry Nataliya." His father had been putting the pressure on and Konstantin had realized that things with Emma were getting too deep.

"And then Tiana died."

"Da." And Konstantin had grieved the loss of his sister-in-law and friend, or so he had believed her to be, but part of him had been relieved.

Because the formal period of mourning meant their father would stop harping on the marriage contract for at least a year.

"Listen, whatever you think of me, believe me when I tell you that the thought of marrying a woman who had a thing for my brother was *never* something I wanted. I was prepared to do my duty, but that's it."

"And that duty had you abandoning the mother of your child," his brother said on a sigh.

"I did not know she was pregnant."

"Of course you didn't. You would never have let her disappear otherwise."

At least his brother trusted him that much. "She did disappear. I think she changed her name because of the restraining order, but I don't know how she managed to hide so well."

"Did she say she was hiding?"

"No, but Emma said she spoke to Tiana." He told his brother what Emma claimed Tiana had said. "It's still hard for me to believe she threatened Emma like that."

Even knowing Tiana had been behind the TRO, Konstantin had believed she was his friend.

"Is that what you said to Emma?" Nikolai asked in a tone that implied a yes answer was the wrong one.

Konstantin experienced a sinking feeling deep in his gut. Because while he *hadn't* said that to Emma. Exactly. He had sort of implied she'd exaggerated Tiana's desire to take their baby away.

"I hadn't spoken to the lawyer yet, Nikolai. Look,

I know you and Tiana didn't always agree on the life-style of a royal, but she was approachable."

"Where I was not?" Nikolai asked stiffly.

"Hell, Nikolai. You took on the mantle of King at twenty-seven. You became my sovereign and the brother relationship didn't feel as real after that."

"I am sorry. It was a hard transition, but it was not my intention to make you think you couldn't come to me. I'm still your big brother."

"And I believed Tiana was my friend."

"I am sorry you had to find out differently. Tiana really did not want to get pregnant. She must have seen Emma's pregnancy as a way out of having to go through one of her own."

"That's like a plot out of a novel."

"You know what they say…"

"Real life is stranger than fiction." Konstantin certainly could affirm that cliché.

"It certainly is, but Konstantin, you have something more important to think about than the melodrama of five years ago. You have gravely insulted the mother of your child on behalf of a dead woman who was not who she pretended to be."

"Gravely insulted?" What was his brother talking about?

"You doubted Emma's word about what Tiana said to her. If I know you, that wasn't the only thing you said that Emma could take offense to."

"I'm not a bad man." Though he hadn't been feeling like a good one since meeting his son for the first time. "She calls him Mickey."

"Mickey is a fine nickname. At least she named him after you."

Konstantin nodded, though his brother couldn't see it. "Giving him my second name was more than I deserved."

"Listen, brother, you are *not* a bad man, but you are a man with *a lot* to make up for."

"You're so sure."

"Since you were a small boy, when you feel guilty, you attack. Even if you did not do that, you broke up with your pregnant girlfriend to marry another woman."

"But it was my duty! And I didn't know she was pregnant." He could wish he had until the end of time, but that would not change the past.

"Which makes you a guy she can trust. It's just going to take her a while to see it."

"I've got a plan for that." He was going to ask her to marry him. What could be a more certain and binding commitment than that?

"Good. Just, be prepared to work for it."

"You don't think I know how to work for something?"

"In business? You'll go without sleep for days and sacrifice your personal time for the good of the company, but you've never worked for a relationship."

"And you have?"

"You know Nataliya. Can you doubt it?"

Konstantin had to smile at that. "No."

"I think this is my fault, even if I didn't have anything to do with the restraining order," Konstantin blurted out as his thoughts finally coalesced on a possible motive for Tiana's actions.

"What do you mean?" Nikolai asked, his voice lacking the condemnation Konstantin expected.

"I told Tiana I didn't know if I was strong enough to walk away from Emma and stay away." He hadn't been.

Konstantin had gone looking for Emma, needing her comfort after Tiana's death.

And he hadn't been able to find his ex-lover. He'd thought about hiring a private investigator then, but that marriage contract had still been hanging over his head. Konstantin had believed it would be unfair to Emma to start something up again only to have to end it again somewhere down the line.

His every good intention had been turned back against him.

Even his recent search for the woman he'd never been able to forget had come up empty. Running into her in the bank had been some kind of miracle.

Which maybe meant not all of his luck was bad when it came to her.

"That does not make Tiana's actions your responsibility. A less ruthless, less manipulative person would have supported you without fabricating evidence for a restraining order you knew nothing about."

Konstantin knew his brother spoke the truth, but he still felt incredibly guilty.

He'd lost out on sharing Emma's pregnancy and almost five years of his son's life because he'd made too many bad decisions, not least of which was confiding in the wrong person.

Emma walked into the restaurant where she had agreed to meet Konstantin and wasn't surprised to find him and an older gentleman at a table already.

The tables on either side were taken up with his

security detail, both for protection and privacy, she would imagine.

The Prince hadn't been thrilled when she'd once again refused to come to his hotel. Emma had stood firm though and Konstantin had eventually given in. Asking where she wanted to meet.

She'd named the restaurant because though Emma didn't often dine out, a friend worked here and Emma knew it would be nearly empty midmorning.

Which it was. Only one other table was occupied across the dining room from Konstantin and his entourage.

The Prince rose when Emma was a few feet from the table and pulled a chair out for her. The table was set for two, the older man sitting in front of a blank spot. A carafe of coffee sat in the center of the table as well as a plate of small sandwiches.

She didn't think this restaurant had sandwiches on the menu. They probably didn't, but the request had been made by royalty. Little chance of it being ignored.

She nodded her thanks to Konstantin and sat down, casting a curious glance at the other man sharing their table.

"Good morning, Emma. Mikhail is well I trust." Konstantin returned to his seat, his attention fully on her.

Even after all these years, it was a heady feeling. One she did her best to ignore.

"Mickey's great." Wanting to see his *dad* again, but Emma and the Prince had some things to work out first. "He's at his preschool day care."

"What does that mean, *preschool day care*?" Konstantin frowned. He didn't like not knowing everything.

There had been a time when she'd seen that as an endearing quality. She had to fight against doing so now.

But nothing about this man could be endearing to her.

"It's exactly what it sounds like," she told him. "A preschool that also offers day care. Mickey has four hours of preschool daily and the rest of the time there he's in the day care portion of the facility."

"How much time does he spend there every day? Does he like it?"

They were legitimate questions. Not really intrusive at all, but Emma had to force herself to answer them. For Mickey's entire life, there had never been anyone else to question, to offer input on her choices.

Now, suddenly Konstantin was here and making noises like he meant to stay in Mickey's life. Which was what Emma wanted, but it was going to be an adjustment for her, on so many levels.

"I work full-time, though I've arranged to work my last two hours each day from home after Mickey is in bed. I also take thirty-minute lunches, rather than the hour the company offers. So, he's in day care about six to six and a half hours, depending on my commute time."

"Your world is arranged around our son," Konstantin observed as he offered her coffee.

She declined with a wave of her hand. "I don't drink caffeine."

She'd cut out all caffeine when she was pregnant and then been encouraged to keep doing so by her first yoga instructor. Since she slept better at night, she had to agree it had been a good, if difficult choice.

"It is. And yes, he likes his day care and preschool," she said, answering Konstantin's questions. "Though

I'd already taught him a lot of what he is now learning, while I was still working as a nanny and had him with me all the time."

Mickey complained sometimes of being bored in his school, but for the most part he enjoyed it and he adored his teacher.

Hence picking up the man's phrases and using them.

"You worked as a nanny?" Even as he asked, Konstantin was texting something on his phone.

"Yes." She saw no harm in telling Konstantin what she'd done in the past. It had no connection to her position as a bookkeeper now. "It allowed me to be with Mickey while giving me the time to take a couple online college courses every term."

"You got your degree?"

"An associate's rather than a bachelor's degree like I'd meant to, but sometimes plans have to be adjusted to work in the life we live."

"That's a very wise attitude to take."

"A necessary one, in my life anyway." She was happy she'd found calm acceptance. At first, she'd resented all the losses in her life, and spent a lot of fruitless time despising the man in front of her.

"You are proud you've taken the upheavals with equanimity," he realized out loud. "As you should be."

"I'm proud of a lot of things, but that's not what we're here to talk about." She cast another glance at the older man who had sat quietly while she and Konstantin talked.

"No. It is not." Konstantin indicated the man. "Emma, this is Albert Popov. He has been on the palace's legal team since he passed the bar."

The lawyer who had drawn up the TRO. He had silver in his hair and the lines around his eyes indicated he was probably in his fifties. So, a long time, then.

"I won't say it's a pleasure to meet you, because I don't know if it will be," Emma said. "But I will wish you a good morning." She didn't know why the lawyer was there, but she suspected Konstantin wanted to hammer out a legal agreement for parental rights and visitation.

"I will try to make our meeting as pleasant as possible." The lawyer gave Konstantin a nervous glance.

Emma didn't trust either man, but she knew she had to hear them out. "Okay."

Konstantin's earlier text made sense as a server approached with assorted herbal tea sachets in a basket and another carafe, this one no doubt filled with hot water. He and Mr. Popov waited while she chose a tea and set it steeping in her cup.

Only then did Konstantin pour himself a cup of coffee, the scent nearly making Emma moan. She missed coffee.

"Albert is the lawyer who filed the restraining order." Konstantin looked at Emma expectantly.

CHAPTER FOUR

EMMA DIDN'T SAY ANYTHING.

He could have chosen a different lawyer to bring to this meeting, but the Prince had never been what she would term *sensitive*.

Konstantin continued to look at Emma like he thought she might start asking questions, or something.

Emma just waited.

"He did not do it on my behest," Konstantin said as the silence stretched.

Oh. So, they were going to discuss the TRO first. Emma did a calming count in her mind. "So you claimed yesterday, but he did do it on your *behalf.*"

"At my former sister-in-law's command, *not mine,*" Konstantin stressed. "He did not consult me before filing the paperwork, nor did he consult me after."

Mr. Popov cleared his throat. "I believed Prince Konstantin wanted the temporary restraining order taken out against you. What I believed to be his testimony about your stalkerish behavior was very compelling."

"Was it?" Emma asked noncommittally. She'd thought the allegations sounded dramatic and over the top.

But then she'd known them to be the lies they were.

"I know now that Her Highness had fabricated the document, but at the time I believed the accusations to be genuine."

"And you never even spoke once about this to Konstantin, I mean His Royal Highness?" Emma had no trouble believing the crazy Queen had instigated the TRO, though she had no clue why. But Emma found it difficult to accept that the lawyer hadn't ever once mentioned it to Konstantin.

"You are the mother of my son." Konstantin reached out and placed his hand over hers on the table. "You always have leave to call me by my first name."

Emma tugged her hand away, tucking it with her other one safely in her lap. Touching from this man was not in the safety zone for her peace of mine. "I'm pretty sure that's *not* how it works."

Konstantin frowned at her withdrawal.

But it was the lawyer who spoke next. "I realize now that it was a grave error on my part, but no, I did not confirm details or intentions with His Highness."

Emma made no effort to hide her skepticism. "I find that incredibly hard to believe."

"I am finding it difficult to credit I was so easily led myself, Ms. Sloane."

"Carmichael," Emma corrected him. "I had to change my name to get a job."

The lawyer gulped. Konstantin's jaw went rigid at the reminder.

"I apologize most sincerely for that, Ms. Carmichael." Mr. Popov loosened his tie at his neck, looking uncomfortable. "His Highness has informed me that

at no time did you stalk him and he would never have
approved the restraining order."

The man's manner was stiff and the words sounded
rehearsed.

Could he be believed?

"And yet you were able to get it in his name," Emma
pointed out reasonably.

Mr. Popov gave Konstantin another nervous glance.
"Our legal team holds power of attorney to do a great
deal on behalf of the royal family. This is to protect
them and their time, you understand."

"My brother and I have now agreed that all POAs
held by our legal team will be reviewed and rewritten
so that nothing of this sort could ever happen again."
Konstantin didn't look nervous. He looked angry.

Really angry. And disgusted.

The lawyer winced.

She didn't imagine the rest of the legal team was
going to be happy to have their purview limited, but
Emma thought the move was long overdue. No one
should be allowed that much leeway with another person's life, no matter how convenient it might be.

"How do I know you are telling me the truth?"
Emma asked, genuinely wishing one of the men could
have an answer for her. "What possible motive could
Queen Tiana have had to instruct you to do such a
thing, even going to the effort of making up supposed
testimony for Konstantin?"

"As to that, I couldn't speak to our deceased Queen's
motives." And the lawyer's tone implied Emma
shouldn't even be speculating.

Like just because Tiana had been a queen, that made
her above having her actions questioned.

Emma wasn't impressed. "Isn't it more likely that Konstantin has convinced you to lie for him so I don't think he's such a rat?" she mused aloud.

Konstantin had to know that the less she trusted him, the stricter the restrictions around his visits with Mickey would have to be.

"Rat?" Mr. Popov asked faintly, his eyes wide.

"I would never stoop to instructing a retainer to lie for me." Offense rang in every syllable of Konstantin's denial.

"Wouldn't you?"

"I have never lied to you, Emma, even when it would have been easier on us both if I had." Konstantin took a breath, clearly collecting himself. "Do you have any further questions for Mr. Popov?"

"No."

"You are sure?" Konstantin asked, like he expected her to change her mind.

"I thought he was here to negotiate the visitation schedule," she admitted. "He's not?" she asked, just to make sure.

"That is something you and I will work out between ourselves." Konstantin's tone left no room for argument.

Emma didn't actually want to discuss her private life with lawyers, but she had the urge to argue just because he was so sure of his own mind *and* hers.

"I have counseled against such a haphazard approach," Mr. Popov said, obliquely reproving the Prince, but not coming right out and doing so.

Emma gave him a wry look. "If what you told me is true, I'm not sure Konstantin should be taking any kind of legal advice from you."

The lawyer looked offended, but before he could say anything else, Konstantin dismissed the older man with a wave of his hand. "Emma is right. You made a grave error in judgment five and a half years ago and every day since by not telling me what you had done. Whether you should remain in our employ is still up for discussion."

The lawyer looked like he wanted to argue, but Konstantin's forbidding expression kept him silent. "Keep your phone on in case Emma changes her mind and wants clarification of anything."

Mr. Popov nodded and stood. "Of course, Your Highness." He bowed toward Emma. "It was a pleasure to meet you, Ms. Carmichael."

As the man walked away, Emma rolled her eyes at Konstantin. "Now, I *know* he lies."

"He is a lawyer, of course he lies, but he's not lying about the TRO."

"I'm sure there are lots of honest lawyers," Emma said rather than revisit the restraining order issue.

Konstantin looked more abashed than she expected from her comment. "I am sure you are right. I spoke out of turn in my frustration."

"And because you are feeling guilty."

"Yes." He frowned. "I am surprised you realized that."

"There was a time I knew you very well, Konstantin." And not just his body. While he'd seen her as a convenient sexual partner, he had been the love of Emma's life.

And she'd paid attention to his every mood. His every reaction. Emma had naively believed they had so much in common.

They'd diverged in one crucial way that really said how very little any of the other aspects of their relationship mattered.

Emma would never have dumped him for the sake of duty.

"I never lied to you, Emma. I told you our liaison was to be temporary. I told you about the contract when I'd never told another person."

"That's not true. Tiana knew."

"As did the rest of our royal family and our legal advisors, but I never told other friends or women I dated."

"Slept with, you mean. You weren't a big dater."

"I dated you."

He had. Not at first, but she wouldn't move into his apartment if he wasn't willing to have at least a semblance of a normal relationship, which meant dating.

Konstantin had insisted they couldn't meet each other's friends and families, but she'd understood his reasoning. He didn't want to be at the center of a media storm when people found out he had a live-in lover.

"You dated me like a married man does his mistress. You were very discreet."

"And you said you understood the need for that discretion."

"I was a naive nineteen-year-old when we met. I fell for you like a ton of bricks and you were from this world I couldn't even fathom." Emma gestured to the restaurant. "Even this isn't really my world. My world is a fixer-upper house that I love, a job that will allow for a trip to Disney World with Mickey once, maybe twice in his childhood."

"But that world, it is no longer yours either."

She sighed. "I know. I'm smart enough to realize

some things will change now you've decided to acknowledge your son."

"It was not a matter of deciding but of knowing about him."

"You keep saying that."

"And you do not believe me." He took a sip of his coffee and stared at her over the rim of his cup, his expression unfathomable.

"What is there in our past relationship or even the present one for me to trust, Konstantin?"

"I broke up with you for the sake of my family and a promise I had made. Doesn't that tell you that at the very least, I keep my promises?"

She wasn't as impressed as he clearly expected her to be. In fact, she barely refrained from rolling her eyes. "You signed a contract, Konstantin. I never doubted how important business was to you." She just hadn't realized that marriage fell under that umbrella for him.

Even after he'd told her about the contract, part of Emma simply hadn't believed he ever planned to follow through on it. Not with the way he treated her. Not with the fact he'd signed it several years before they'd met and had never even dated the woman named in it, Lady Nataliya Shevchenko.

"Which was a commitment I made on behalf of my family and myself."

"It was a draconian agreement," Emma condemned.

Konstantin laughed, though there was little humor in the sound. "That is what Jenna says."

Tension stiffened Emma's spine. "Who is Jenna?"

"Nataliya's best friend."

"Is she your girlfriend?"

"No, of course not. I do not do girlfriends." He

pinned her with a dark brown gaze. "You were the single exception."

That might have meant something if he hadn't dumped her. "Latest sex partner, then."

"No. I think my youngest brother would gut me if I made a play for Jenna. Not that I see her giving him the time of day, but that is not the point." Konstantin smiled, inviting her to share the joke.

Emma was all out of humor at the moment. Finding out he had a son might be every bit as easy for Konstantin as he was making it out to be, but Emma's entire life was changing.

Again.

Because of this man. Again.

The truth was, they'd veered completely off topic and it was her fault. "I believe the point you were *trying* to make is that since you keep promises to your family, I should trust you to keep any promises you make to me."

"Yes."

"I'm not sure if it has escaped your notice, but first, that was a business contract, even if family was involved. And two, I am not your family and you betrayed *me* pretty spectacularly in the past."

"How did I betray you?" he asked, like he really didn't know.

"You dumped me, but that wasn't enough for you. You evicted me completely from your life so I could not even reach you. You allowed your crazy-pants sister-in-law to have a TRO taken out on your behalf that made my life that was already imploding even worse. You let her threaten me and my role in my unborn child's life."

"I did not know about any of those things!"

"But if you had not cut me from your life with such precision, you would have. Now you want me to believe that *if* you had known, you would never have let any of that happen. It's a reach, Konstantin."

"I had no choice."

"Did you even try? Did you go to your father or your brother and say, hey, can we renegotiate that medieval contract so I can stay with this woman I fancy?" Emma didn't use the word *love* because he never had.

"You know I did not. You make it sound easy, but it would not have been. Nikolai took over his responsibilities as king decades before he should have had to. I could do no less than what was required of me for the sake of our country and my family."

"Which meant what? You had to marry a woman you did not love?"

"Love did not come into it."

"No, it didn't. Not for you anyway." He had never even come close to loving her. She saw that now, but she'd loved him. So much, she'd grieved his loss even after she thought he'd taken the TRO out against her.

"I did not love you," he acknowledged. "But I was obsessed by you. When I said I had no choice, I wasn't just talking about the contract."

She hoped he didn't think she was flattered to have been his *obsession*. An obsession was an object, not the target of genuine emotions.

"If not the contract, then what?" she asked.

"I knew that if I did not cut you completely from my life, I might not be able to stick with the breakup."

"You underestimated yourself. You broke up with me without looking back."

She'd been devastated, her heart shattered by the realization that all the emotion she had been feeling had been entirely one-sided.

No, he'd never lied to her, but his actions, his intense passion, it had all convinced her younger, more naive self that his emotions were growing just like hers had been.

Emma had been devastatingly wrong.

"That's the problem. I did look back. Too many times. And Tiana knew it. Although, I knew nothing about the restraining order, I think I know why she took it out."

"Why?"

"She was protecting me from myself."

"Because you told *her* that I was your obsession."

"Yes."

"And, good *friend* that she was, the crazy Queen lied and connived to take out a TRO on your behalf." Unfortunately, from her limited exposure to Queen Tiana, Emma had no trouble believing that.

Though she didn't think the woman had been protecting Konstantin. "She would have had her own reasons for taking out the TRO. I doubt very sincerely that woman ever did anything altruistically."

"Why do you call her crazy? You have so much antipathy for her."

"She threatened to steal my child." Did he not get how serious that was? How awful and terrifying that threat had been to a twenty-year-old who hadn't had the resources to fight a custody battle with a normal person, much less a monarch? "Sure she wrapped it up in legalese, but the end result would have been her taking my child to raise as her own."

"That is a side of Tiana I never saw, but I believe you."

"Do you really?" That would be a volte-face from the day before.

"Yes." Nothing but sincerity rang in his tone.

"Well, that's something."

"Perhaps you could extend a little belief to me as well."

Emma searched her own heart. Did she believe he hadn't known about the temporary restraining order? The answer was more complicated than simple belief or denial. "I spent more than five years believing you were cruel and callous enough to take out the TRO."

Changing her viewpoint of him wasn't going to happen in a single conversation.

"And that shames me because you are right. Ultimately, it was my fault."

Emma could not disagree. "I am willing to entertain the idea that you did not have anything directly to do with that. I'd rather believe that to tell the truth. I hated the idea that Mickey had a giant rat for a father."

"Maybe just a small rat?" Konstantin tried teasing.

She shrugged, not kidding herself.

Even without him being the source of the TRO, Konstantin had treated Emma badly and it had taken her a while to realize that it was his fault and not hers. She hadn't brought the pain down on herself. Innocence wasn't stupidity. And being trusting was not a defect in her nature, but a strength. One that might cause her pain in the future as it had done in the past, but she would rather have pain than spend her life thinking everyone was a liar, or worse.

"You made unspoken promises to me with your ac-

tions," she told him now, revealing an understanding
that had come with a lot of soul searching and reading some very wise self-help books. "You implied a
level of intimacy and even commitment that we did
not have with how much you seemed to need me. Do
you understand that?"

"But I told you our relationship was temporary."

"That first week we met, when you told me about
a contract that was already years old, but you never
mentioned it again. Not when you insisted we live together, not when you made sure we spent as much
time together as possible. You called me when we were
apart. You treated me like I mattered. Until I didn't."
Just like her parents had.

Although they had been strict, they had been loving and kind. Until she disappointed them and they decided they didn't want her as their daughter anymore.

"The contract was always there, hanging over my
head. I never forgot about it."

Even when he'd been calling her in the middle of
the night just to hear her voice when he'd been out of
town on business, or duties with the palace. She believed him because right now, the anguish in his tone,
it was genuine.

He'd felt conflicted. Just not conflicted enough to
remind *her* he didn't plan for them to stay together,
she told herself.

They could not change the past, but she had learned
from it. Perhaps he had as well.

"What now?" she asked Konstantin. "Mickey isn't
going to be happy seeing you only a few days a year,
but I don't imagine you come to New Mexico often."

She really had no idea what Konstantin had meant

the day before when he said he was staying in Mickey's life. As a secret father who saw their son sporadically? As a public dad who made an effort to see Mickey once a week?

The options and what they would mean to her own life had kept Emma up the night before.

"I come to Santa Fe, once or twice a year," he said dismissively. "Surely what comes next is obvious. Naturally, we will get married."

It took Emma's brain several seconds to parse what Konstantin had said because it was so out of the realm of what she had been expecting. "Married? You and me?" She grabbed one of the goblets of water from the table, not even sure it was hers, and gulped it down. "You don't mean that."

"If I had known about Mikhail before he was born, we would be married already."

"Now, I know that is a lie." And she'd just started to buy the whole "I will never lie to you" shtick. At least in words. "There was still the contract."

"And it would have held no weight when compared to my impending fatherhood." He sounded like he truly believed that.

Emma wasn't as convinced, but neither of them would ever know because she had not been allowed to tell him the truth about her pregnancy and then she'd been well and truly scared off by a queen's threat to take away Emma's baby.

"You haven't asked for a DNA test." Which was a point in his favor. "You thought he was yours from first sight."

"He announced his age quite loudly. There was no chance in my mind that little boy could belong to anyone but me. Besides, he looks just like me." Konstantin sounded really proud of that fact. "As for a DNA test, *I* do not need one. I'm sure at some point the palace legal team will require DNA proof before my brother names Mikhail as part of his succession line."

"Mickey? In the succession to the throne. No. That can't be right. We weren't married when he was born."

"We will be married and he will be legitimized through all proper channels."

"I never agreed to marry you." And honestly? Right now, she could not fathom it.

Emma had no intention of putting her heart on the line with this man again.

"You agree that Mikhail needs me in his life."

"Yes."

"More than once or twice a year."

"Yes." It would mean moving and that would be really hard, but for Mickey's happiness, Emma would reshape her dreams again. "Do you still make your primary home in Seattle?"

"You do not follow news of me?" he asked again trying to tease.

He used to tease her all the time, but their relationship wasn't what it had been.

"Don't be an egoist. Just answer the question."

"I spend equal time in Mirrus and Seattle with business trips on behalf of Mirrus Global once or twice a month." He frowned, like something about that schedule bothered him.

"Okay. So, I'll relocate to Seattle," she said all in one breath, getting out the words that were so hard to say.

Her family still lived there even though they no lon-

ger acknowledged her. Maybe that could change. She
could not imagine anyone being able to reject Mickey.

"You're willing to move?" he asked, surprise lacing his tone.

She did roll her eyes then. "You thought marriage
was the solution to our situation. I assume that would
have required me and Mickey to move."

"Well, yes, but…" His voice trailed off, the Prince
seemingly without words.

"Will it be hard?" she asked. "Yes," she answered
herself. "If you want the truth, it's going to be awful.
I'm not just proud of the life I have built for me and
Mickey, but I love it here. I fit in *The City Different*
better than I have ever fit anywhere else."

"You will fit in our life in Seattle and Mirrus. I will
make sure of it."

"I think that is something I have to make sure of,
but thank you."

She sighed. "Look, I'm not so naive as to think
you're going to change your base of operations just to
be closer to your son, even if right now you're all gung-
ho about the fatherhood thing." Konstantin was not that
guy. "If I have the option, I want Mickey to have both
of us in his life on a consistent basis."

Or as consistent as a prince could be in the life of
his son. As yet, Emma didn't know what that was going
to look like, but she did know that Mickey's dream of
family had the best chance of coming true if she lived
in the same city as his father.

That was the truth that had kept sleep so far from
her the night before.

"You're a very special woman."

"No. I'm just a mom who wants what's best for her

child." Emma didn't think that made her special, just committed.

"Mickey having both his parents is very important to you isn't it?"

"Do you really need me to answer that?"

"Enough for you to marry his father and give him a complete and stable home life?" Konstantin asked leadingly.

"He can have stability without us marrying."

"I can legally acknowledge him as my son, but the world is not as forward-thinking as we all might wish. There will be many who will not give him his due unless I am married to his mother."

"This isn't the Dark Ages." But she knew Konstantin was right.

"No, but we do not live in a perfect Utopia of understanding either."

She took a fortifying sip of her peppermint tea and wished it was a peppermint mocha, loaded with caffeine. "You don't want to marry me."

"That is one thing about which you are absolutely wrong."

"But why?" He had never loved her.

Permanent had never been in the cards for them, no matter what fantasies she'd woven around their relationship in the past.

"You are the mother of my child."

"I never thought you were such a throwback."

"Didn't you?"

Okay, maybe when he'd jettisoned his mistress to marry the woman chosen by his family, Emma had thought a Neanderthal playboy might be a step up from

Konstantin, but this? Marriage? "You don't think I'm wife material."

"You have given birth to my child and raised him to the best of your ability, sacrificing in ways many women would not. You are eminently suitable to be my wife."

She shook her head. "You might even believe that right now, but spend a couple of hours talking to your family and your attitude is going to change fast enough."

"Not true. I told my brother I planned to marry you and he's all for it."

"Right."

"I will never lie to you, Emma, and I will keep reminding you of that until you believe me."

"Your brother the King is supportive of you marrying a bookkeeper?" she asked disbelievingly.

"Artist-slash-bookkeeper, but yes he is. His advice was to be willing to work for it."

"I find that hard to believe. You always said your brother was a stickler for propriety and you marrying your former mistress who gave birth to a child, even if it was *your* child, outside marriage isn't it."

"I have come to appreciate that my view of my brother was skewed by Tiana and my friendship with her."

Emma mulled that over. "I don't think Tiana was the friend to you that you believed her to be."

"Her wanting to buy my son and raise him as her own says you are right."

In a twisted way, the Queen might have thought she was protecting Konstantin. Emma found herself saying just that.

"No. With the TRO, maybe, but threatening you? Wanting to take our child? That was never about friendship."

"You knew her better than me. I only spoke to her once."

"And then you ran fast and far."

"Not intentionally. My parents had kicked me out. I needed a job right away but the TRO was making that impossible. I couch surfed with friends and started the proceedings to change my name. Once it came through, I started applying for nanny positions again. One of the positions was for a family that was relocating to New Mexico. I did some research and realized that the cost of living here would make raising Mickey on my own easier."

"So, you took the job."

"I did. Tiana died in her skiing accident the month after the move. I was already heavily pregnant and had no intention of moving back home. I couldn't be sure she was the only one in your family who felt the way she did about separating me from Mickey."

"She was. My father and brothers were all appalled when they learned what she threatened you with."

"That is good to know." She sighed and said what needed saying. "Five years ago, I would have married you without hesitation."

"Are you saying now you are hesitant?"

"I don't love you anymore, Konstantin." A twinge in her heart said she might be lying to herself and to him, but she ignored it. "I don't trust you. I cannot imagine marrying you."

"And I cannot imagine any other future for either of us."

"You're going to have to work on your imagination, then."

"We shall see."

He was so arrogant!

"I will compromise my dreams for Mickey's sake, but I'm not marrying for anything but love. I won't compromise on that."

"Then I will just have to rekindle your love for me."

"As difficult as that would be, even more impossible would be convincing me that you feel the same way for me." Emotionally done, Emma stood up. "Look, when you're ready to discuss visitation with Mickey in a rational manner, give me a call."

He surged to his feet. "I was trying to do that."

"Throwing around the idea of marriage like it's a panacea is not being rational. Marriage is a lifetime commitment. At least for me."

"For me as well."

"So, just stating we're going to get married when we don't know if we can even spend a full day together in harmony is ridiculous."

Konstantin reached his hand out toward her. "You and Mickey have dinner with me tonight, please."

"You eat dinner too late for Mickey." Her voice sounded harsh to her own ears, but she was compensating for how that *please* made her feel.

His Royal Highness Prince Konstantin of Mirrus did not plead.

"I will eat whatever time is good for his schedule," Konstantin promised without hesitation.

She nodded, believing him. "We eat at five thirty." That was practically lunchtime for Konstantin.

"I'll be there at four to visit with him."

* * *

Konstantin brought a croquet set with him to visit his son and Emma. It was the first sport he'd learned as a child. A precursor to training for polo. His second had been skiing, a natural sport for an island country that had snow so many months out of the year.

"You do it like this?" Mikhail asked as he swung the mallet at the ball.

The croquet ball went careening across the small courtyard.

Konstantin smiled. "That was a good, strong hit, Mikhail. Well done."

Mikhail beamed and Emma smiled with approval. She was dressed in what he considered her bohemian Southwestern chic again. He was developing a real thing for turquoise and silver.

"Do you want to come to the park with us tomorrow?" Mikhail asked Konstantin. "It has water fountains. It's lots of fun, right, Mom?"

"I'm sure your dad is going to be busy tomorrow," Emma said gently. "He's here on business, Mickey."

What she did not seem to grasp yet was that no business could take precedence over Konstantin's newly discovered family.

"You don't live here now?" Mikhail asked, his face falling like an express elevator on its way to the ground floor. He turned to Emma. "Mom, he doesn't *live* here! He's going to go away, like Mr. Jensen."

"I am not leaving you, Mikhail," Konstantin promised, dropping to his knee beside his son. "I have just found you. You are my very precious son. We are family."

"Mr. Jensen went away from *his* family," Mikhail said accusingly.

"Who is Mr. Jensen?"

Mikhail didn't answer. He threw himself at Emma, wrapping his arms around her and burying his face in her stomach. She hugged their son, but looked up at Mikhail. "Mr. Jensen is my former employer. He traveled a lot for business and the year before Mickey and I moved out, he left the family to be with a woman he'd met on one of his trips."

Konstantin tapped Mikhail's shoulder. "*Moj mal'chik*, look at me...please." That word again. Pleading with his son and his former lover was becoming a habit. "I am going nowhere. I want no other woman but your own mama, Mishka. I promise you. Now that I have found you both, I will not leave you."

Mikhail turned around to face Konstantin, but held on to his mother. "What did you call me?"

Konstantin had to think, to remember what he'd said, his brain scrambling to keep up with the emotional upheaval. He had known his child for two days and it gutted him to see the little boy upset.

"I called you *my boy* in Russian." He ruffled Mikhail's hair. "And Mishka is like your mother calling you Mickey."

"Okay. I like Mishka better than Mickey, but Mikhail is best." The little boy gave Emma a significant look and she shrugged back.

Like they'd had this discussion before and she wasn't giving up *Mickey* anytime soon.

"But you don't live here," Mikhail said accusingly, showing he had not forgotten his worry in his curiosity. "We do."

Konstantin looked up at Emma, feeling helpless in a way he never did.

Emma's expression wasn't her usual confident, calm mom face. She looked just as lost as he felt.

Although she had said she was willing to relocate, they had made no firm plans. He had not even told her that he was scheduled to return to Mirrus the next day. Not that Konstantin planned to go, but he did not know realistically how long he could stay in Santa Fe.

Until Emma agreed to move, his heart insisted while his brain said that was not practical. He had business commitments.

But the little boy looking at him so warily trumped even Mirrus Global.

Emma dropped down so she was eye level with their son as well. "Listen to me, Mikhail Ansel Carmichael."

Mikhail nodded, then said in an aside to Konstantin, "She only uses my whole name when she's really serious."

Konstantin had a wholly inappropriate urge to smile, despite the emotional upheaval and gravity of the moment. He suppressed it. "So, we must believe what she says, then."

"I always believe my mom," Mikhail said with more loyalty than truthfulness.

Konstantin had seen in their brief time together that the boy's curious nature made him question nearly everything he was told about the world around him.

Emma gave their son a gentle smile. "Maybe not everything, but asking questions is not a bad thing. In this though, I need you to trust me."

"Okay, Mom."

"Konstantin is *your* dad and no matter where any of us lives, no one can take that from you."

"But I don't want him to live far away."

"I know you don't, sweetheart."

Their son grimaced at the endearment.

"I do not want to live far away from you either," Konstantin assured him.

"Are you going to move here?" Mikhail asked innocently, wholly unaware of how costly such a thing would be.

"I would if I could," Konstantin answered, meaning it.

Emma gave him a searching look, as if trying to read Konstantin's sincerity.

But he wasn't worried. He knew all she would see was honesty. If it meant being with his son, he *would* move anywhere. That did not change the truth that his active royal role as Prince and chief operating officer for Mirrus Global precluded him living just anywhere without letting down a lot of people.

Emma stood. "This conversation calls for lemonade."

"Homemade lemonade? The kind with mint leaves floating in it?" Mikhail asked his mother with enthusiasm. "It's the best," he assured Konstantin.

"Would I make it any other way? I have a pitcher I made last night. I was saving it for dinner, but I think we can all use a cool drink right now."

And something to put a smile on their son's face. Konstantin saw the motive to Emma's suggestion. It had worked, though Mikhail took both his mother's hand and Konstantin's, holding on tightly as they made their way into the brightly lit kitchen with its colorful tiles.

Emma was going to hate his home in Seattle, not to mention his apartment in the palace. The designer he'd hired had done both in elegant neutrals.

Apparently, the time had come for a change.

"Sit down at the table with your dad. I'll get the drinks," Emma instructed their son.

"I can help," Mikhail said, even as he obeyed, sitting down so that he would have Konstantin on one side and Emma on the other once she joined them.

"I've got it." Emma smiled reassuringly at the boy and gave a silent instruction to Konstantin to sit down with a nod of her head toward one of the chairs.

Konstantin found himself obeying as quickly as their son had done. Amused with himself, he chuckled softly.

"What's funny, Dad?"

"I don't usually get told what to do," he said with a smile.

"Cuz you're a prince?" Mikhail guessed.

"Yes."

"I think you better get used to it. Mom is bossy."

Emma's laughter said she hadn't taken offense at their son's pronouncement.

"Your mother has always had a way of getting me to do as she wanted," Konstantin told Mikhail conspiratorially.

"Not when it counted," Emma said under her breath.

But he heard her. Konstantin gave her a look that he hoped conveyed his regret for their past.

She just shook her head and carried a tray laden with a pitcher of lemonade and glasses to the table. Konstantin noticed that though his cup matched the two glasses, Mikhail's lemonade was served in a plastic cup that was sized for his smaller hands.

There were so many details in Emma's home that showed she took their son's needs into account in even the smallest of minutia.

Konstantin took a sip of his lemonade and was surprised at how perfect the flavor was. Not too sour. Not too sweet and the mint gave it a refreshing twist. "This is very good. You made it?" he asked Emma.

"Well, me and the lemonade juicer."

"She used to squeeze all the lemons by hand," Mikhail offered. "But it made her hand sore, so Mrs. Jensen bought her a juicer thing."

"I thought you were the nanny, not the housekeeper?" Mikhail asked.

"I had some light housekeeping duties."

"Like making juice?"

"And the beds. I used to help Mom make 'em. She said when I was a baby I helped too, keeping her company."

The idea of the mother of his child doing such menial tasks for another did not sit well with Konstantin.

"I know that look on your face, *Prince* Konstantin, but normal people make beds and juice and clean up after themselves and others all the time. Working for the Jensens allowed me to finish school and stay with my son until he was old enough for preschool day care. It was good for both of us."

"You have provided my son with a stable and good home life," Konstantin said, once again feeling the weight of guilt at the knowledge that she should never have had to do that alone.

"Our son, and it was my privilege to care in every way for Mickey. It always will be."

"Mom says being a mom is the most important and bestest job ever."

"Best," Emma corrected with a smile.

"Best," Mikhail parroted.

For just a moment, Konstantin had no words. This little family was his, through no great feat of his own, or even one good choice after the one to date Emma. This amazing woman had made a future he never thought to have possible.

Marriage to a woman he genuinely wanted and parenting a son who was already a wonderful little human.

Something of what he was thinking must have shown on his face because Emma's expression softened, but then she took a breath and her *no-nonsense* look came over her lovely features. "Mickey... *Mikhail*," she stressed. "Do you remember when you asked about your dad the first time, and I said that when you got to meet him, you might want to move to be near him?"

Konstantin knew that Emma had not planned for that day to happen anytime soon.

"You mean me and you move, right, Mom?"

"Yes, of course. You aren't going anywhere without me." And that was said with rock-solid certainty along with a warning look toward Konstantin.

As if he would ever try to take Mikhail away from Emma. "It is my hope, Mikhail, that your mother will agree to marry me and we can build a family together, but even if she does not," he said quickly when his son opened his mouth to speak and Emma looked ready to clobber Konstantin, "I am hopeful that you will both be willing to make your home in Seattle and Mirrus as I do."

"Two places?" Mikhail asked, sounding confused. "You can have two houses? Is that real?" he asked his mother.

Emma nodded. "Yes, some people have even more than two houses."

Konstantin was one of them, but he didn't mention that right now. His son had enough to process with the idea of living in two locations.

"Is Mirrus your country?" Mikhail asked. "Only Mom said it was an island and you're a prince there."

"I am a prince wherever I am, but it is my country."

"Oh. Mom only called you Prince when she was annoyed with you."

"You could tell that, huh?"

"Yep."

"Your mom doesn't have to call me Your Highness."

"Why?"

"Because you are my son and she is your mother."

"I do not believe that is protocol," Emma said drily.

"But it is the way it will always be between us."

"If Mom marries you, will she be a princess?" Mikhail wanted to know.

"She will, yes."

Mikhail's expression fell. "Oh."

"You do not want your mother to be a princess?" Konstantin asked, trying to understand.

"She doesn't want to be a princess," Mikhail said glumly.

"She told you this?"

Mikhail nodded, tears filling his eyes. "She won't

marry you and we can't be a family." He jumped up and ran from the room.

Emma rushed after him and Konstantin followed. He found them in his son's room, Mikhail refusing the comfort of his mother's arms.

"You won't let us be a family!" the little boy cried.

"That is enough." Konstantin spoke firmly, needing to stop their son's blaming his mother. "Your mother never said we could not be a family."

"But she did," Mikhail said to Konstantin tearfully. "When I asked her about my dad."

"I told him things hadn't worked out between us, but that was okay because I never wanted to be a princess."

"Give me a chance to convince her otherwise," Konstantin said to Mikhail.

"My mom is really stubborn. When I don't want to do something good for me, she tells me that she's more stubborn than me cuz she's been stubborn longer." Mikhail looked so forlorn.

"If that is how it works, then I must be more stubborn than she is because I am four years older than she is, so I have been stubborn longer. And I am a prince. That means I am used to getting my own way."

Mikhail's expression lightened, but Emma looked like a thundercloud.

"I love you more than anything in this world," Emma said to Mikhail. "But, sweetheart, I am not marrying your dad just to make you happy."

She sounded so sure, but suddenly Konstantin suspected that she probably would do that very thing. It was clear that nothing was more important to Emma than Mikhail.

It was Konstantin's job to show her that their becoming a family legally, because they were already a family in truth, would *not* be at the cost of her personal happiness.

He would show both her and Mikhail what kind of life they could have together.

CHAPTER FIVE

"YOU BOUGHT A HOUSE? Here?" Emma asked faintly, not sure she'd heard Konstantin right. "But why? I told you I would move to Seattle with Mickey."

"Eventually," Konstantin clarified. "And I think we will be returning to Santa Fe more than twice a year. It is a place that you love."

She ignored the way he talked like she and Mickey would travel with him and focused on her son.

They had spent the last week together more than she would have thought possible with Konstantin's schedule. It had become obvious to them both, from small outbursts to having trouble sleeping and disturbing dreams that sent Mickey into her bed for a cuddle, that their son needed time to adjust to all the changes in his life.

"But we discussed the move and you agreed Mickey needed time to adjust to having a dad before we uprooted him." She'd been relieved that Konstantin hadn't fought her on that.

Because Emma was self-aware enough to know that *she* needed time to come to terms with having Konstantin become part of Mickey's life as well.

Emma had gotten Mickey a counselor to help him

with the transition but wondered if she shouldn't have gotten one for herself as well. She'd been almost as shocked when Konstantin had offered to attend any family sessions as she was right now.

"You can't do your job from Santa Fe." Could he?

"I will do it to the best of my ability, but naturally some adjustments will have to be made both in my palace schedule as well as my responsibilities as COO." Konstantin sounded way too calm about that, considering what a workaholic he was. "My father and brothers will be stepping into the gap and we are promoting someone to work directly under me in a managerial capacity."

"But…all that…so Mickey and I don't have to move right away?" He was putting his precious business second?

He was allowing others to fulfill his palace responsibilities?

Konstantin had never done that when they were dating. Though he'd been very respectful of her time, his had always been in short supply.

"You both have a life here. Mishka will be graduating from preschool in a matter of weeks. It would not be fair to take him away from the teacher he admires so much before the natural separation of him moving on from preschool."

"I agree." Only Emma's plan had been for her and Mickey to stay in Santa Fe until then, while she put her house up for sale.

The prospect of finding a home in Seattle to move to was daunting. She would have to find a job there as well. There was just so much to do.

Overwhelmed by what it all meant, Emma pushed

her food away. Konstantin had asked to meet for lunch so they could talk without upsetting Mickey. She wished she didn't have to be part of this conversation either.

It was just all so much. She'd worked so hard to build her life here in Santa Fe and now she had to dismantle it.

Sometimes, she wished she could go back and deny, deny, deny. Only that was impossible now. She'd been the one to insist on having a paternity test done. She wasn't having anyone question Mickey's parentage.

Whom was she kidding? She would never have denied Mickey his chance at having his dad in his life. No matter how hard that change might be for her.

Konstantin looked at her with concern. "It is my hope that you and Mikhail will move in with me, getting him used to having me around while staying in Santa Fe."

"What?" Move from her little house? The one *she'd* bought with no help from anyone else?

"Surely you can see this would be for the best. The counselor said that taking steps like this could help Mishka settle."

"I don't think she was talking about us moving in with you. We can help Mickey adjust to having you around without living with you." Couldn't they?

"Even if you refuse to marry me, surely you see that you and Mickey living with me would be the best course of action. Once he is introduced to the world as the new second in line to the throne of Mirrus, he will require a level of security that a place of similar size to your current home could not accommodate."

Emma couldn't deny it. Konstantin had already implemented security measures at her house that had required putting a portable bed in the living room for the night shift. That was not a tenable long-term solution.

"I can get a bigger house." But she'd looked at Seattle real estate. Even after selling her current home, she wouldn't have enough of a down payment to get anything bigger than a two-bedroom condominium. No yard for Mickey.

"I will buy you whatever size house you require, but I would prefer my son live with me."

"Which means me living with you." Nothing Konstantin had said implied he had any plans to try to take Mickey away from her, but she could not help worrying.

"Naturally. I would prefer as my wife, but yes, regardless. Whatever you feel about this truth, our son *is* a royal and he must be raised to his role. It will be better and easier for him if he lives that life 24/7."

Why hadn't she ever considered Mickey's role within the royal family? Because after her confrontation with Queen Tiana, Emma had realized she was on her own with her son. Even before that, she never would have expected Konstantin to formally and publicly acknowledge him.

"Which means living with you."

"Yes."

While she had never expected him to take this step, part of her *had* been afraid Konstantin would try to take Mickey away from her. Emma had not trusted the Prince at all. Not after the restraining order and the Queen's threats.

So, this idea of living with him had *never* occurred

to her and Konstantin talked like it was the most natural thing in the world.

Emma had become convinced that she'd never really known Konstantin. That the man she'd fallen in love with did not actually exist.

The jury was still out on that one, but his every action right now pointed toward a man who had no plans to try to steal her son away. Even so. "I know you are used to getting what you want, but can't you see you're asking me to change my whole life for you?"

"For Mikhail," Konstantin stressed. "After treating you as I did, I would never presume to ask you to change so much as your outfit for me."

"What's wrong with my outfit?" she demanded.

Her Prince blew out a frustrated breath. "Nothing is wrong with your clothes. They look fantastic on you as always."

Darn it. She'd thought of him as hers. She had to nip that in the bud right now.

Only did she? asked an insidious voice in her mind, or was it her heart? He wanted to marry her. Wouldn't that make him hers?

"Then why would you want me to change them?" she asked rather than let herself dwell on impossible thoughts.

If princes rolled their eyes, then Konstantin would have done so right then. She was sure of it.

His gorgeous lips twisted wryly. "I am *not* asking you to change them. Although, if I felt I had the right, I would point out that you might consider letting me buy you a designer wardrobe for public functions."

"Why would I be attending public functions with you? We aren't dating."

"That is going to change."

"What?" Why were they talking about dating now? Hadn't they been discussing her moving into his Santa Fe mansion?

"We are going to date."

"Not if I don't want to." Only she wasn't entirely sure she *didn't* want to.

No matter what Emma said, she could not ignore her son's happiness and desire to live as a "real" family. Nor was she in the habit of lying to herself, which meant she was fully aware of how attracted to Prince Konstantin of Mirrus she still was.

In the past week, her view of Konstantin had changed.

Although she was still very hurt by how he'd cut her so ruthlessly from his life, she no longer held him responsible for the restraining order that had caused her so much grief.

Konstantin had gone in the opposite direction, taking on a load of guilt that he freely acknowledged.

Both situations served to give her a less jaundiced view of her Prince. Oh, darn it, she'd done it again.

"Why are you frowning?" Konstantin asked.

"You are *not* my prince," she told him and herself.

His smile was sexy and devastating. "But I could be."

She just shook her head.

"I spoke to the counselor and she believes that having you and Mishka move in with me here in Santa Fe, letting us get used to being around each other as people who live in the same home while he still has the consistency of his preschool, would be good for our son."

"You spoke to the counselor about it? Before me?"

"Only to get her opinion. Naturally, it is your decision entirely."

Not really. Not anymore.

While Emma had no plans to give up majority custody of their son, so long as he continued to make Mickey's welfare a priority, she expected Konstantin to have a say in Mickey's present and future. While she would not allow him to dictate decisions about their son, she *would* take Konstantin's viewpoint into consideration.

Even if she didn't feel so strongly about allowing him to fulfill his role as father, so long as he did so with Mickey's best interests always at the forefront, the simple truth was Konstantin knew the intricacies of royal life in a way Emma did not.

Mickey needed his dad looking out for him and Konstantin was doing his best to do that very thing.

Emma needed to remember that.

"I don't want to move out of my home," she admitted baldly. "I know I have to, but I worked so hard for Mickey and me to have our own place."

"Would it be easier for you if I moved in there for a couple of weeks?" Konstantin offered.

Like that was practical, but she did appreciate his offering. "Where would you sleep? The kitchen?" she asked facetiously.

"We could put a travel bed in your bedroom with a standing divider between us."

It was a generous offer. They would be crowded beyond belief, but he was willing to do that so *she* had time to get used to moving from their home, not just Mickey. Only she wasn't a four-nearly-five-year-old.

Emma was an adult and she could deal with the hard things in life.

She'd already proved that to herself many times over.

"I think it *would* be good if you stayed with us for a couple of days before we made the move to your mansion," she said, giving oblique acceptance to the move to his mansion and by extrapolation to a shared home in Seattle.

"I never said it was a mansion."

She gave him a look. "Is it?"

"Yes." His teasing smile invited her to share his amusement.

She returned it. "I know you better than you think."

"I don't mind that."

"Can we get an RV to park in my driveway for the security people?" Then she would have some semblance of having her home back again.

"That is an excellent idea. I should have thought of it already."

"You've been busy." She knew he had.

Konstantin worked late into the night most nights just so he had time every afternoon and evening to spend with Mickey. She joined them for most of that time because Mickey needed that sense of security.

However, Emma had continued to do her job and paint her commissions for the gallery as well.

Which meant as soon as Mickey went to bed both she and Konstantin began work on their computers. He'd surprised her by staying to work in her living room until she went to bed some nights. She wasn't sure why he did it, but Emma acknowledged, if only to herself, that she liked it.

* * *

Konstantin brought his things from the hotel and Emma made room in her closet for his suits.

The prince planned to sleep on the travel bed they'd brought in for the night security man.

She gave the single bed a considering look. "Have you ever slept on a single bed?"

"Not since being in the nursery." Konstantin shrugged. "The bed was good enough for my security man, it is good enough for me."

"I wouldn't expect that attitude from you."

"Why not? Because I am a prince?" he asked her with a slight frown. "Believe me, I have slept in much less comfortable surroundings."

That really surprised her. "You have?" He certainly hadn't while they were together.

"Indeed. I did my service in our military just as every Mirrussian must."

"You mean every Mirrussian male."

"No. Every citizen of Mirrus must serve at least two years in the military between the ages of eighteen and twenty-six."

"But what about pacifists?" she asked.

"There are many military roles that do not require combat readiness."

"Oh. And your citizens are allowed to choose?"

"If they swear a pacifist's oath, they are placed in a noncombat role."

"And you trust them not to take advantage?"

"It has worked for the two centuries of our country's existence."

"That's kind of wonderful."

"I am glad you think so. Mirrus is a very special place."

"You would think that," she teased.

She'd used to tease him about his absolute conviction there was no better country to live in than Mirrus.

"I hope you will agree." His smile said he was sure she would. "You and Mikhail will be living there for several months out of the year."

"If I say," she reminded him, but acknowledging in her own heart that he was right.

She hadn't come out and formally agreed that she and Mickey would live with Konstantin, but she accepted that it was most likely inevitable.

Mickey *was* part of the royal family.

Which, even now, sort of blew her mind.

"If you say." The words agreed with her, but his expression said Konstantin knew what was what.

"You know, even back when I realized I was pregnant and tried to get a hold of you to tell you, it never occurred to me that you would want to recognize our child officially."

Konstantin frowned. "What did you think I would do?"

"Well, you'd made it pretty clear you *didn't* want to marry me," she pointed out. "So, I thought you'd help with his support and do visitation, I guess."

"It was never that I did not want to marry you. I never even allowed myself to consider the possibility. I believed I had no choice about marrying Nataliya."

"And yet you claim you would have married me if you knew. Saying stuff like that makes it harder for me to trust you now." Did he get that?

"Why? If it was true?" he asked, his brows drawn in confusion.

"But how *could* it be true? You put that contract ahead of our relationship from the beginning to the end. You want me to believe that me being pregnant would have made a difference, but I have very bad memories just trying to get a hold of you to tell you I *was*."

"And that was my fault. I acknowledge that. You tried every way you knew, I understand that now." The words were too stilted to be rehearsed.

He meant his belated apology and acknowledgment that Emma had done all that *she* could.

"Good."

"And then you spoke with Tiana and she scared you with her demands and threats. You should never have been subjected to that," Konstantin said like he was intent on getting it all out at once.

"On that we agree completely, but how is this supposed to convince me that if you knew I was pregnant, you would have walked away from that contract?"

"Because Mikhail is my son." He said it so simply, like that explained everything.

"So, shared DNA trumps family and business commitments?"

"That shared DNA means Mikhail is my family, and in my world, he's the most important member of that family."

"Your child is more important to you than your brothers, even the one that is King, or your father?" she asked, pushing for clarification, not sure she believed Konstantin about that claim.

However, if she was going to put her life in his hands, as it were, by agreeing to live in his space, she needed to know that Mickey came first and her own role as Mickey's mother would never be diminished.

"Yes."

Emma looked at Konstantin, trying to see into his soul for the truth. But she wasn't that gifted. "You did put everything on hold for him now," she acknowledged.

"I cannot stay here forever," Konstantin said, almost apologetically. "But I will make his transition into the world you think of as so foreign as easy as possible."

She frowned, but nodded. Konstantin's world was foreign to her and to Mickey. In so many ways.

"I think I want a contract with you," she mused, coming on a solution she would not have considered to be a benefit a week ago. "A shared custody agreement that guarantees my role as full-time mother to Mickey no matter what the future holds. And I want final say on all major decisions regarding him for at least the next year."

She needed to see Konstantin being the father he promised to be before she handed over any legal rights over Mickey.

Konstantin's brows drew together, his expression clearly unhappy. "You want a contract between us?"

"Yes."

"But our relationship is not business."

"Right now, it's not personal either." She should not have said *right now*. It implied she would be open to a personal relationship later.

And Emma just didn't know if she was. Even if she agreed to marry Konstantin, she wasn't sure how personal she was willing to be with him. Emma had never once considered a marriage of convenience as a possibility in her life. She'd grown up dreaming of marrying her soul mate, like her parents were to each other.

But then, she'd never really considered what it would mean if her son's father, who was a prince, showed up in their life either.

It had never occurred to her that they might just run into each other. She'd thought that when Mickey was older she'd have to help him get in touch with his father.

This situation? Had never even been on Emma's radar.

So, she hadn't planned for it.

"You are the mother of my son. You are the only woman I have ever lived with. How much more personal can it get?"

"That was years ago. We don't live together anymore."

Konstantin looked around them significantly.

"Not like that. We aren't sleeping together."

"Not yet."

She glared at him. "Don't count your chickens, Your Highness. They're likely to fly the coop."

"What does that mean?" he asked, humor evident in his tone. "You are not a chicken."

"Neither am I a sure thing for you and you'd best remember that. You are *here* for Mickey's sake, not because I want you sharing my space."

Later, as she tossed and turned in her empty bed, images of her ex-lover on his own narrow cot kept her from sleeping.

Konstantin was the only man Emma had ever had full-on sex with. Her parents had been overprotective, and Emma had had a strict curfew when living at home.

After she and Konstantin had broken up, she'd been

too devastated to date. Then Emma had found out she was pregnant. Her life since Mickey's birth had only recently had *any* time that might be used for dating.

But Emma had been gun-shy. Her one relationship had come at a high cost to her. She wasn't ready to trust someone else and she'd never been as attracted to another man as she was to Konstantin.

She knew *he* hadn't been celibate. He was discreet, but even discreet, there was gossip about his sex partners. Not lovers, because like he said, Konstantin did not date. Nor did he live with other women.

Even so, when Emma had seen the fashion articles about Lady Nataliya's dates, Emma had been sure that they would infuriate Konstantin.

Emma was probably one of a very few who had not been surprised when Nataliya had ended up betrothed to his brother the King. Konstantin could be a throwback and she had no doubt he'd reacted poorly to Nataliya dating in such a public way.

Emma admired the Princess of Mirrus and her refusal to adhere to royal expectations, even though, if she were completely honest, Emma would have to admit she had also been jealous of the woman and her role as Konstantin's intended.

Now, Konstantin said he wanted to marry Emma. For Mickey's sake.

Which was really nothing like his actually *wanting* to marry her.

She supposed it wasn't that much different for him than agreeing to marry Lady Nataliya as part of a business deal.

But Emma had always dreamed of marrying her

soul mate. At one time, she'd thought Konstantin was that man.

Now, she didn't know what to think.

And it wasn't making sleep any easier to come by.

Mickey was over the moon to have his dad at the breakfast table, though Konstantin had been up for a few hours working already.

Emma knew that because she'd heard him get up a full two hours before her own alarm was set to go off.

She'd been so tired from her sleepless night, she'd just rolled over and gone back to sleep, waking to the smell of breakfast sausage, coffee and a distinct lack of an alarm. She'd found her phone missing from her bedside table, only to discover it on the kitchen counter when she arrived.

Konstantin and Mickey were both seated with plates of yummy-looking breakfast foods in front of them.

"Did you cook breakfast this morning?" she teased her son.

"No, Dad got some people to deliver it. It's good, Mom. You'll like it."

Emma picked up her phone and checked the time, frowning when she realized if she didn't hurry, she wouldn't make it to work on time. "I'm going to be late."

"I called and told them you had been unavoidably detained." Konstantin didn't look guilty about being so high-handed either.

"After you took my phone and made sure I didn't hear my alarm?" she asked with a grimace.

His own frown censured her. "You were sleeping soundly. You clearly needed your rest."

"That wasn't your decision to make."

"When do you plan to give notice at work?" he asked, ignoring her rebuke.

"I already put in my notice." And she'd started looking for a new job in Seattle, but she was beginning to wonder how that was going to work with them traveling to Mirrus every few months to stay for weeks at a time.

"Good." He dished up her plate. "Our son told me your favorites."

Emma took the plate of eggs ranchero and crispy hash browns with a polite thank-you. The food smelled so good, her mouth watered. And then her stomach rumbled.

Mickey laughed. "You're hungry, huh, Mom? It's good you don't have to wait to cook your food, right, Mom?"

"Yes, Mickey." She leaned down and kissed her son's head. "Very good, especially since we need to leave very soon to get you to school on time."

The first hour at Mickey's day care preschool was free time so children could be dropped off at different times before the morning preschool session started.

Mickey's mouth set in a mutinous frown that was becoming all too familiar. "I don't want to go to school. I want to stay with Dad."

"If it is all right with your mother, I can pick you up right after school so you don't have to go into day care," Konstantin offered, obviously intent on heading off a confrontation with their son. "But I too need to get some work done today."

Emma didn't know how she felt about the Prince's offer.

So far, all of Mickey's time with Konstantin had

been under Emma's supervision. But a man didn't go to the trouble of setting up a mansion to live in if he planned to run off with her son, did he?

It all boiled down to whether, or not, she trusted Konstantin at his word that he would not try to take Mickey from her.

"Say yes, Mom, please!" Mickey pleaded.

Emma looked at Konstantin, and his chocolate brown gaze so like their son's snagged hers. His eyes asked her to trust him. "I…"

She didn't know what to say. Could she take Konstantin at his word?

He was right when he claimed he'd never verbally lied to her. Would he start now?

He had to know that if he tried to take Mickey she could make such an ugly scandal, his little country would be in all the wrong papers for months to come. Would he risk that?

She closed her eyes for a moment, centering herself, and sought the truth of her own emotions and beliefs.

"Don't worry, Dad. She does that sometimes. It helps her focus on what's real." Mickey sounded so grown-up repeating her words for Konstantin.

Emma opened her eyes and smiled at Mickey. "Okay, but you call me at work as soon as your dad picks you up." She looked at Konstantin. "If you want to take him to the park or something, you need to call and let me know you aren't going to be at home."

It would be only for a couple of hours, she reminded herself. He needed just the one to disappear with their son, but she wasn't going to think like that.

"Of course," Konstantin replied, his expression

filled with a vulnerable gratitude she did her best to trust. "And thank you, Emma."

"For what?" But she knew. They both knew she was showing more trust than he probably deserved right now.

But she realized she was trusting her own judgment more than she implicitly trusted him.

"Trusting me with our son."

Emma just nodded.

CHAPTER SIX

KONSTANTIN PICKED UP Mikhail from his preschool, impressed by the security employed by the staff.

Despite traveling with an entourage and his obvious wealth, as well as being greeted by the bodyguard that had been watching over his son since Konstantin came into Mikhail's life, Konstantin was still required to show photo identification.

He also heard one of the staff calling Emma to tell her that Mikhail was being picked up. Though he knew that she'd taken time to go into Mikhail's preschool and arrange things so the Prince could pick up his son.

"You must be Mikhail's father. We've heard a lot about you in the last two weeks." The dark-haired man speaking looked to be a couple of years younger than Emma's age of twenty-five. He extended his hand. "I'm Jerome Leeds, Mikhail's teacher."

Now, Konstantin understood his son's insistence on being called by his given name. It's what the teacher he admired so much used.

Konstantin shook the younger man's hand. "It is a pleasure to meet you. I have heard a great deal about you as well."

Jerome Leeds smiled. "We aren't supposed to have

favorites, but I have enjoyed teaching Mikhail very much."

"He likes Mom too. Lots," Mikhail said guilelessly.

Stiffening, Konstantin gave the teacher a look meant to intimidate and wasn't even a little ashamed to do it. "Is that right?"

"Yep. I think he wanted to date her, but Mom doesn't date." Mikhail frowned.

Konstantin didn't like the idea that his son might be disappointed Emma had refused to date the other man.

"I'm sure she had her reasons," Konstantin told his son. "Are you ready to go?"

Mikhail's sweet little-boy face lit up. "Yes! Where are we going?"

"Nowhere until you call your mother and check in with her."

"Oh, right." Mikhail turned back to his teacher. "See you tomorrow, Mr. Leeds."

The man, who was now showing every evidence of embarrassment, nodded. "See you tomorrow, Mikhail."

"I'll tell Mom *hi* for you like you always ask."

Mr. Leeds gave Konstantin a defiant stare and said, "You do that, Mikhail."

Konstantin took out his phone, dialed Emma's number and handed the instrument to his son.

He waited until Mikhail was engaged with his mother before saying to the teacher still standing there, "You are aware that the mother of my son is no longer available for dating." Though from what Mikhail said, she'd never made time for it.

Konstantin hadn't dated either, but he hadn't been celibate the last five years and suddenly, he regretted that. He didn't know why. He'd been single. He'd never regretted having casual sex on Nataliya's behalf.

Their contract had spelled out very clearly that until a formal betrothal announcement was made there were no personal obligations between Lady Nataliya and any of the Princes of the House of Merikov. Konstantin's father, King at the time, had signed on behalf of their house and the contract did not stipulate Konstantin personally.

Though both families had expected him and Nataliya to marry one day, it had been an unwritten obligation and one that did not carry with it the burden of fidelity to a relationship that did not exist.

Regardless, now he wished he'd handled a lot of things differently the past five years, not least of which was cutting himself off completely from Emma.

"Does she know that?" the preschool teacher asked. "Only a man who wasn't there for the first few years of his son's life isn't a great bet and I'm sure she knows that."

"That is none of your business." Konstantin knew he *was* a good bet and Emma would come to learn that as well.

That was all that mattered.

Jerome Leeds frowned. "I care about Mikhail."

"And I am glad to hear that. He deserves to have the people in his life care about him," Konstantin said honestly. "But he and Emma are *my* family. As long as you understand that, we will have no trouble between us."

The threat was there and Konstantin did nothing to soften it.

"Just don't hurt her again," the teacher had the temerity to instruct him. "She's a special person and I think you must be the reason she was so closed off to dating. She deserves to have the people in her life care about her too."

The younger man was speaking about things that he had no right to even mention, but Konstantin did not disagree with what he said. So, he chose not to take umbrage.

"She does." Konstantin smiled at his son as the young boy finished talking to his mother. "As I said, they are *both* my family and I will watch out for them now."

"That's good to know, Mr. Merikov."

Konstantin didn't correct the other man's address. He rarely felt the need to point out his royal status. He knew who he was. Random strangers, or even his son's teacher who would be in that capacity for only the next few weeks, did not need to.

"It's Prince Konstantin or Your Highness," Mikhail said, showing he was not so sanguine about the issue. "My dad is a prince."

The pride in Mikhail's voice touched Konstantin deeply. Unlike with Emma, apparently Konstantin's royal status was a check in the plus column for their son.

"Is that right?" Jerome Leeds asked indulgently.

"It is," Konstantin affirmed. "Now, if you will excuse us."

He put his hand out for his son to take and then led Mikhail out of the school without looking back to see how the news was received.

"Dad, how come Mr. Leeds didn't know you are a prince?"

"Perhaps because your mother did not think it was important to tell him."

"Oh. Because she doesn't want to be a princess?"

"I think because my role as Prince is less important to her than my role as your father. She told them about that, right?"

Mikhail brightened. "Yep. Where are we going?"

"Where would you like to go?"

"The park!"

Because he had accompanied Mikhail and Emma to the park twice now, Konstantin knew exactly where Mikhail wanted to go. Konstantin gave instructions to the driver and then called Emma to tell her where they were going.

The bodyguard riding with them engaged Mikhail in conversation while Konstantin was on the phone.

"I should have guessed that would be where you ended up. Given a choice, it's almost always the park." There was a smile in her voice.

"It would seem so."

"Mickey is really excited you picked him up today. He told me other kids had more than one person who picked them up and now he did too." She sounded a little sad and maybe wistful.

"You and Mishka will never be alone again," Konstantin vowed. "Not only will I always be there, but my father, brothers and sister-in-law are all very eager to meet my son and his mother."

"I don't know how I feel about meeting them. Queen Tiana told me that she had her husband's full support to take Mickey, and that of her father-in-law as well."

Konstantin didn't like the worry in Emma's tone.

He assured her, "She told you she had my support too, but we both know she lied about that."

Silence met that statement.

Konstantin waited, wondering if Emma would agree, ignore or deny his words.

"She did," Emma finally said with a sigh. "About a lot of things."

"Yes, about many things. My father and brothers learned about Mishka only after I met our son."

He couldn't wait for Mickey to meet Dima, his youngest brother. Both his brothers would be wonderful uncles, he was sure, but Dima was the youngest and had a special place in Konstantin's heart.

He looked to make sure Mikhail was otherwise engaged. His son was now playing a game on the bodyguard's phone with a set of headphones so he could hear his music without interrupting Konstantin. Konstantin nodded his thanks to the other man.

"I have not yet told you how grateful I am that you chose to continue your pregnancy and when you did that you did not choose to give Mishka up for adoption. Your strength inspires me."

"That's a nice thing to say, but my parents would have burned my name in effigy if I'd terminated my pregnancy," Emma said with dark humor. "Not that I ever considered doing so. I don't know. I just loved Mickey from the moment I knew I carried him. If I'd been able to give him up for adoption, Mom and Dad would not have disowned me. They thought I was being selfish toward them and him by keeping him."

Konstantin hated that this amazing, generous woman had lost her family just when she'd needed them most. "I never realized they were so unbending. I knew they were angry you'd moved in with me because you told me, but not that they would reject you for having a child without the benefit of marriage."

She sighed. "They were always strict, but I thought they loved me enough to forgive me for making choices they would not agree with."

"Perhaps it was a matter of believing *tough love* would bring you around to their way of thinking."

"Maybe." Emma didn't sound convinced though.

"Have you tried contacting them since having Mikhail?"

"I did when Mickey was a month old. I wanted them to meet their grandson."

"What happened?"

"My mom asked me if I'd kept the baby and I said yes. I started to tell her how beautiful he was, how amazing, but she hung up on me."

Konstantin had some very uncharitable thoughts about her parents. Whatever their reasoning, they had hurt her terribly with their rejection of Mikhail.

Not that he'd done any better on Emma's behalf, if unwittingly, but going forward that was going to change. Full stop. "I am truly sorry to hear that. Once we are married, they will no doubt accept you again. You will have to decide if that is something you want."

She gasped. "I never said I would marry you." Emma's tone was all sass.

And Konstantin loved it. Why when Nataliya read him the riot act did he get nothing but annoyed, but when Emma took him to task, he found it more than a little attractive?

She was right, of course. Emma had in fact stated she would not marry him, but Konstantin wasn't giving up. Apprising her of the fact didn't feel like the next smart move, so he remained silent.

"I will be home in a couple of hours. Will you and

Mickey be there?" Emma asked in an obvious effort to change the subject.

"We can be, or you can have an hour to yourself while I take him to the Children's Museum."

"You'll wear him out." Her tone was filled with warmth.

So, Konstantin didn't take the complaint seriously. "Mishka has an infinite source of energy."

Emma's laugh went straight to his libido. How had he gone so long without hearing that particular sound?

"I know it seems that way," she warned him. "But you'd better make sure he gets a snack, or you'll see how quickly that energy goes to the dark side."

"Noted."

"I've got to get back to work."

"Yes."

Neither hung up. It reminded him of the times they used to just sit on the phone and listen to each other breathe when he was out of town on a business trip. Their words would run out, but their desire to stay connected would not.

"This is... I..." Emma sounded lost. "I have to go." And she hung up.

But she'd felt it too. He knew she had.

Emma pressed End Call and dropped the phone like it was a snake.

That had been... That had been way too much like the way things used to be. For just a moment, she was living in the place where she still loved him, where she'd thought he'd actually cared about her, where her very being hung on the next word he said and knew his hung on hers.

She'd suffused with desire so intense, she'd lost sense of reality. For a moment, she had disconnected with her air-conditioned office with its perfectly uniform plants and cubicles for the other three bookkeepers.

It was the moan that she could feel making its way up her throat that brought Emma back to the present.

She'd told Kon she had to go and hung up before she did something crazy like ask him to come get her too.

Predictably, Mickey was too tired to do much playing outside after dinner.

He wanted a movie night on the sofa with Emma and Konstantin.

"I can sit with you, but I need to do some work on my computer," Konstantin told their son.

"Okay, Dad. Thanks for taking me to the park and the Children's Museum today. It was lots of fun." Mickey yawned.

"But now you want to relax. It is good you recognize what you need."

"Mom says that if I'm feeling cranky, I need to look inside and try to know why."

Smart mom, but everything Konstantin observed between Emma and Mikhail told him she was an exemplary mother. "Oh, were you feeling cranky?"

Mikhail shrugged. "Tired."

Konstantin nodded. "Sure. I'm a little tired myself," he admitted.

"But you still have to work?"

"I do." Konstantin swallowed his own yawn.

Emma came into the room carrying a big bowl filled with popcorn, which she placed on the coffee table. "You two get settled. I'll get the lemonade."

"What movie would your mom like?" Konstantin asked Mikhail conspiratorially.

Mikhail brought up their streaming service on the smart TV. He clicked on a family movie about a princess who saves herself. "She likes this one."

Naturally. "Your mom is a strong lady who can take care of herself just like this princess." However, it would be Konstantin's pleasure to care for Emma's needs going into the future.

"Only Mom isn't a princess."

"But she would make a good one, don't you think?"

"Like this princess?" Mikhail considered. "Yeah, maybe."

"I agree."

"What are you two agreeing about?"

"You're like this princess, Mom." Mikhail snuggled in next to Konstantin.

Emma sat on the other side of their son. "Am I?"

"Definitely," Konstantin answered as their son took a handful of popcorn and tried to shove all the kernels into his mouth at once.

He shook his head and smiled at Emma.

She grinned back and shrugged. "What can I say? He likes popcorn."

Mickey wasn't the only one who had been craving more family, Emma realized as she relaxed with her son and the man who had been her only lover.

She used to dream of simple evenings like this, her and Mickey cuddled on the couch for a relaxing evening in with the man in her life. That guy hadn't had a face in her dreams, but his body had been suspiciously like Konstantin's, his skin the same tone, his hands strong and capable.

She'd never dated, too burned by the double rejection of the man she loved and the parents she adored to risk putting Mickey through anything similar.

But this? Felt right. Too right for a man who had ejected her from his life like dangerous waste.

Maybe she had been dangerous to him.

By his own admission, Konstantin had found it hard to stay away from her. However, he'd been determined to keep his commitment to that darn contract. He hadn't even tried to renegotiate it.

That was the sticking point that Emma found hardest to get past.

So, he *hadn't* taken out the TRO, or even known about it.

He *had* broken up with her and made it impossible for her to reach him to tell him about her pregnancy.

He *had* left her vulnerable to Queen Crazy.

But he *hadn't* broken his word where the contract was concerned. Maybe King Nikolai was right and she *could* trust Konstantin on some level. Oh, not as *her* family. Not even if she did eventually agree to marry him. But if he would sign a contract like the one she'd suggested, maybe she could trust he would be committed to sticking to its terms.

Konstantin had shown that when it came to putting his name on a document, her Prince took that seriously. When he made a legal commitment, he kept it.

Predictably, after his busy day, Mickey fell asleep halfway through the movie.

Emma stood to lift him, but Konstantin beat her to it. "Time for bed, I think."

"We'll both regret it if you don't take him to the bathroom first."

Konstantin did as she suggested, helping their sleepy son with a prosaic acceptance she would not have expected. They got him into his pajamas together and then tucked him into bed.

"What?" Konstantin asked as they came back into the living room.

She turned off the movie, wanting to talk without Mickey overhearing more than she wanted to finish a movie she loved, but had seen many times. "I just… You're really good at that."

"Am I? I worry that I'll do something wrong and hurt him without meaning to." Konstantin moved into her personal space.

Emma stepped back. "You're a really natural father."

"I had a good role model." Konstantin gave her a challenging look as he sat on the middle of the couch, leaving the only spot beside him.

The armchair had been moved to make room for the bed and wasn't ideal for sharing a conversation with someone on the sofa.

"Your father?" Emma bit the bullet and sat beside him, her body hugging the arm so their thighs did not touch.

Emma needed to focus for this conversation and she was fully aware that Konstantin in close proximity would not be conducive to that focus.

"Yes." Konstantin relaxed against the sofa, laying his arm across the back, mere inches from her shoulders. "He was a king first, I always knew that, but he was a good father, interested in my brothers and me, involved in our lives from infancy."

"How could you know that?"

"Dima is nearly eight years younger than me. I got to see my father with him as a baby. Nikolai has always been a hands-on older brother too. I let myself forget that when he became my sovereign," he said, his expression introspective. "Both of them modeled what being a good father-slash-caretaker looked like."

"I guess I thought you'd been raised mostly by nannies."

"We had nursery staff, but my parents were always the last word in discipline and the first to give us the affection every child needs."

"That's why you're so comfortable hugging and playing with Mickey." Which had surprised Emma from the beginning.

As long as she'd known him, Konstantin had always kept a physical distance from others. It was like he walked around with an invisible barrier surrounding him.

When they were together, he'd invited her inside that barrier, touching her all the time. Which had been another reason she'd mistakenly thought she was special to him.

"The only people I have ever been comfortable touching are my family, and later you," he said as if inside her brain and responding to her thoughts. "As I got older, a natural distance developed between me and my family."

And he'd created a world's worth of distance between him and her when he broke up with Emma.

"Or maybe once you lost your mom, you all sort of pulled into yourselves instead of relying on each other for comfort," Emma mused, ignoring the obvious about their own lack of physical closeness.

Konstantin shrugged. "Perhaps. I was fifteen, and I wanted to accept her death like a man."

"But you weren't a man. You were still a kid." Her heart hurt for the teenager he'd been.

"Dima was the one who was still a child. He needed us all to be strong for him." Konstantin smiled indulgently at her. "Do not look as if I am sharing the great tragedy of our age with you. I never stopped hugging my little brother when he was a child, if that makes you feel better."

Dima was an adult now, finished with university and starting graduate school.

"It does." Taking a deep breath, she said, "Something else would make me feel even better."

"I have a feeling it is not the same thing that I am craving."

Suddenly the air around them was heavy with sexual energy.

Emma tried to concentrate on the flow of air in and out of her lungs, but it didn't stop her nipples beading to almost painful peaks and vaginal walls from contracting with a need she'd ignored since being thrust from his life.

"I'm pretty sure you are right," she acknowledged in a tone that was way too breathless for her liking. "Have you thought about signing a contract like I asked about last night?"

"Why?" he asked, sounding pained.

Forcing herself not to react emotionally to his obvious hurt, Emma drew on her own sense of certainty. "You never once even considered breaking that marriage-slash-business contract when we were together. You see your legal obligations as absolute."

"Not absolute. I broke the contract last year, when Nataliya humiliated me in the media." He didn't sound particularly proud of that fact.

"Did you?"

"I was feeling guilty and angry."

"That's never a good combination for you."

"No, it is not. It is how I ended up cutting you off so completely."

"What were you feeling guilty about then?"

"You were a naive nineteen-year-old when we met. A virgin. And I didn't care. I wanted you."

"So you've said. You were obsessed with my body."

"I was that. I wanted you all the time, but Emma, even more dangerous to my commitments was the truth that when I was with you, I was happy."

"So happy that you dumped me. Let's not rewrite history."

"I am not trying to rewrite anything." He blew out a clearly frustrated breath. "I am trying to be honest."

"Okay, so in all honesty, you dumped me because you had committed to marrying another woman in a contract."

"Yes."

"You want me to trust you with Mickey. You want to be his dad. You want us to move in with you."

"I want you to marry me."

"But I am not there. I may never be there. What *I* need is to know with as much certainty as I can have that I can trust you not to try to usurp me with my son. That even if I never marry you, you will not attempt to take Mickey from me."

"My word is not enough for you?"

"No." She swallowed, knowing she wasn't done, and he wasn't going to like her next request any more than the first. "I would prefer that your brother the King sign the contract as well."

"Why?"

"Because your former Queen took out a TRO against me on your behalf. I need to know that your current monarch will not do anything like that."

"He never would."

"You didn't think Queen Crazy would either."

"No, I did not. And the truth is I misjudged both my brother and my deceased sister-in-law. He cares for me far more than I thought, and she was no friend to me at all."

"I would agree, at least with the latter."

"You'll see that Nikolai is a good man."

"If he is, then he won't mind signing the custody agreement."

Konstantin frowned. "This is really important to you, isn't it?"

"I want to trust you, Kon. You don't know how much. I see how important you already are to our son, how keenly he misses having an extended family, but I'm his mom."

"And no one will ever try to take that away from you," Konstantin promised fiercely.

"So, sign the contract. Get your brother to sign it. Give me something to trust."

"I am not enough."

"Stop saying that. Don't you see that you doing this shows me that you're as committed to Mickey's happiness and my safety as you claim to be? This would be *you* being enough. This would be *you* being trust-worthy in the way that *I* need it."

The only question was would His Royal Highness's pride allow him to follow up all his verbal promises with action?

Konstantin grabbed his phone and dialed. "I have a task for you," he said into it rather than a greeting. "I need a custody agreement that guarantees Emma's role as primary custodian of our son, regardless of any other circumstances. In addition, you will include a proviso for financial support." He named a monthly sum that was ridiculously high. "The palace will take responsi-bility for security for both Emma and Mikhail."

The man, Emma thought it was probably the law-yer she'd met earlier, Albert Popov, squawked at the other end of the phone.

"That is not your decision to make," Konstantin re-plied.

The man said something else.

Konstantin's expression turned iceberg cold. "And why would I take *your* advice on matters of this na-ture after your colossal error in judgment regarding the TRO you took out on my behalf against the mother of my child?"

Emma could not hear what the lawyer said, but she now knew for sure it was Mr. Popov. Konstantin re-laxed just a tiny bit, so whatever the man had said, it must have been conciliatory.

"There needs to be a place for me to sign, but also my father, my brothers and my sister-in-law." Konstan-tin frowned. "I am quite sure I know how my family will react to being asked to sign this agreement bet-ter than you do."

Mr. Popov said something else.

"*Da*. Have the paperwork officially recognizing Mikhail as my son ready to sign." Impatience lined every inch of Konstantin's face. "We have already done the DNA testing."

Emma had insisted on it that first week and now she was glad.

"Yes, it was Emma's idea. But there was never any question I am Mikhail's father." He said this to Emma, though she was sure the lawyer thought Konstantin was talking to him.

Konstantin gave the lawyer a couple of more directions that would put definitive protections for Emma's role in Mickey's life in place and then ended the call.

"Do you have a lawyer to look these papers over?" he asked her.

"I…no. I'll have to get one." She would use the rainy day fund she'd been saving for the house's repairs and remodel. "Thank you for that. You did more than I expected. Are you really going to get your whole family to sign the agreement?"

"Yes."

"But will they?"

"Yes."

"You're so sure."

"Mikhail is my son."

"You said he was next in line after you in the succession for the throne. I… Doesn't that mean King Nikolai wants a say?"

"I have just found out that Nataliya is pregnant."

"Which is really great for them, but doesn't change anything about Mickey's role in the monarchy until that child is born."

"Nikolai is a good man. He will understand your desire for the contract."

"Yeah, but he has to trust me in order to sign it," Emma said as that truth literally hit home with her. "How can he? He doesn't know me."

"He knows me. I trust you. He either trusts my judgment, or he does not."

"And if he doesn't?" she couldn't help pushing.

"Then Mikhail will stay with you in the States when I travel to Mirrus."

"Just like that? But that isn't what you want."

"I will do what I have to do to ensure you trust me to fulfill my role to Mikhail as his father without ever compromising your role as his mother. From the moment I learned of his existence, you and he became my priority."

"But that's not how it works, is it?"

"I lost you once to my responsibility to the crown. I will not lose you, or my son, again."

She was sure the nearly five years of life he'd lost with Mickey was the deciding factor for Konstantin, but even knowing how very much he regretted that helped Emma to trust Konstantin in Mickey's life.

If not her own.

CHAPTER SEVEN

DESPITE HIS ASSURANCE his brother and the rest of his family would sign the agreement promising not to interfere with Emma's parental rights and role as Mikhail's mother, Konstantin wasn't at all sure they would.

He and Nikolai had lost trust in each other since their mother's death. There had been a time they were best friends, despite their age difference, but they'd grown apart.

Now, Konstantin realized that they had both handled their grief at the loss by turning inward. Their father had done the same. The only person any of them had continued to show affection for had been Dima and even their youngest brother had eventually pulled himself into his own space and life, away from them all.

Nikolai's marrying Nataliya had brought a lot of warmth back to the palace and Konstantin realized that the same could not be said of his brother's first marriage.

Tiana had not been the friend Konstantin thought she was, but worse she had been a poor queen and an even worse wife. He'd been blinded to the truth, but he wasn't anymore.

He was learning to trust Nikolai's judgment again, but was his brother doing the same for Konstantin? He would soon find out.

Nikolai remained silent on the other end of the phone as Konstantin explained what he wanted his brother to sign and why.

"She said this would help her trust you with Mishka?" Nikolai inquired.

"Da."

His brother made a thoughtful sound. "Is she refusing to move to Seattle without it?"

"Nyet, but that is not the point."

"No." He could almost see Nikolai nodding to himself. "The point is you want her to trust you."

"Da."

"Convincing a worthy woman to marry you is no easy task."

"It is not," Konstantin had to agree. "I am not at all sure I will convince her that marriage is the best solution for our future, even with Mishka on my side."

"I have confidence in you, brother. Even if you were not a prince, you would be a catch."

Konstantin was secretly pleased by his brother's words, but only said gruffly, "So you will sign the custody agreement."

"You are giving a great deal of power to her without any checks."

"It is the same power she would have had if I had not run into her and my son by accident in that bank."

"And some would deny the existence of miracles."

"I would not have thought you believed in them. You have always been so practical." A young king, Nikolai had not had room in his life for impracticality.

"Nataliya is my miracle," Nikolai said, all sincerity, no humor. "She could have married you and I would have been stuck pining for the rest of my life."

"So, I am forgiven for not fulfilling the contract earlier?"

"Forgiven? I will name my firstborn after you in gratitude."

"Nataliya will have something to say about that."

"Yes, she will." Nikolai sounded very satisfied by the knowledge his wife was no pushover.

"Nataliya will like Emma."

"Nataliya likes most people."

"That's a whopper of a lie. Your wife is charming and a fantastic princess, but you and I both know she barely tolerates most of our country's nobility."

"That is true. However, she's an excellent judge of character, so I am sure she will like your Emma."

Konstantin only wished Emma *was* his. "You must think I am a good judge of character to say so." Since his brother had never met Emma.

"You were the one who recognized Nataliya carried a torch for me and that marrying her would be a travesty for both of you."

"But despite that, I never backed out of the contract."

"No, your sense of duty was too strong. And it cost you greatly. Don't think both Father and I aren't aware of that."

"I thought Tiana was the one who cared about my personal happiness, not you," Konstantin admitted.

"She was very good at pretending to be someone she was not."

"Emma isn't like that. What you see is what you get."

"Now that we know her name and whereabouts for the last five years, I've had her investigated." Nikolai spoke with an uncharacteristic caution.

"So, that is why you trust my opinion of her."

"No. I trust you because you are trustworthy, Konstantin."

"That is good to know."

"You must have been satisfied by what the report on her activities told you."

"You know she worked as a nanny for a family by the name of Jensen."

"Yes. She wanted to continue her education but stay with Mikhail until he was old enough for preschool and found a way to do it by becoming the nanny and sometimes housekeeper for the Jensens." Konstantin made no effort to stifle the pride he felt in Emma's resourcefulness in his voice.

"Mr. Jensen was a total womanizer, but she maintained a distance from him when others did not. That marriage was not a happy one before he left."

"That is unfortunate, but Emma would never mess around with a married man."

"No, she would not. I think before she met you, no one would have thought she'd live with a man before marriage either." There was subtle censure in Nikolai's tone.

Konstantin did not take offense. "She was entirely innocent, but I ignored the treasure she was and pushed her out of my life."

"For the sake of a marriage contract you should not have been asked to sign. If Mother had been alive, you wouldn't have. She believed in the modern monarchy."

"Father still has some very old-world views."

"Yes, but he regrets the years he has lost with his grandson because of it." Nikolai paused and then said, "I'll sign the custody agreement, brother, and make sure Father, Dima and Nataliya do as well."

Relief washed over Konstantin. "Thank you."

Emma got advice from the director of Mickey's pre-school day care for a good family law attorney.

She really liked the fiftyish woman who had a solid reputation in family law. The older woman told Emma that the contract was very generous in mone-tary terms—which Emma had already realized—and that while she was surprised, she was happy to see that it was heavily weighted in Emma's favor in regard to parental rights.

Again, it was as Emma had expected, but hearing there were no hidden caveats that might compromise her role in Mickey's life was reassuring.

Though provision for Konstantin's visitation with their son was one area that gave him more than usual access.

Emma didn't mind. She'd agreed to the terms he'd asked for before the contract had been drawn up. She *wanted* him in Mickey's life.

However, the lawyer's last words stayed in Emma's head.

"He's still a prince. And you are still, as you have said, a normal person. A healthy dose of caution is in order. This isn't a fairy tale, but your life with your son."

The attorney's advice stayed in the back of Emma's mind even as she and Mickey prepared to move into Konstantin's Santa Fe mansion.

Mickey had only a few weeks left of school, during which she was hoping her empty house would sell quickly.

She and Konstantin had yet to talk about where they planned to live in Seattle. Partly because she was avoiding being alone with him.

It wasn't that she thought the discussion was unnecessary. In fact, it was starting to eat away at her sense of inner peace not to know where they would be living come summer.

It was just that her attraction to him was growing and Emma was finding it harder and harder to keep her hands to herself and her libido under control when she was around Konstantin.

"You want my room right next to yours?" Emma asked, her voice going high.

They'd come to Kon's mansion for a couple of hours every day to ease the transition of moving for Mickey, but today was her and her son's official move-in.

"You do not like the room?"

"Of course I like the room." It was more than twice the size of her old one, but whether the house had come this way or Kon had made it happen, her room had all the bright Southwestern patterns and colors that Emma liked so much.

But everything, right down to the towels in the en suite bathroom, was high-end and luxurious. The bedding was new and had the discreet logo of a top designer. The furniture was the same.

No pieces found at a garage sale and refurbished for this mansion.

And yet the designer had managed to make the royal residence feel like a home and not just a showplace.

Emma sighed. "It's a gorgeous room. I just don't understand why I'm right next door to you. Won't that cramp your style?"

"Did you just ask me that?" Kon's tone was heavy with offense. "You know I am not seeing other women. My plan is for us to marry."

"I… That's not what I meant." She bit her lip, looked around and dredged up a smile for him. "I'm sorry, okay? I don't know what I mean." Just that being so close to him was going to play havoc on her efforts to keep her attraction for him under control.

But that was not his problem. It was hers.

Kon's intense brown gaze searched her face, his own expression giving nothing away. "Mikhail will feel more confident with both of us only across the hall from his own new bedroom."

Emma couldn't argue that. "You're right."

"So?"

"So, this is fine." She sighed internally, trying for gracious. "Better than fine."

"Good. Mikhail and I have a surprise for you." Kon's smile took Emma's breath and did some very interesting things to other parts of her body that she did her best to pretend were not happening.

Their son chose that moment to knock loudly and then come careening into the room. "Mom, Mom… Wait till you see what Dad and me did. You're gonna love it!"

Grateful for the timely interruption, Emma's smile for her son was a lot more natural. She allowed him and Kon to lead her downstairs. She thought they were going to the outdoor pool, which Mickey was over the moon about, but they turned down the hall in the back and stopped at an open door, clearly waiting for her to go in first.

What she saw took her breath away. Floor-to-ceiling windows looked out over the beautifully landscaped grounds, the lush outdoor pool area off to the right.

The view and the size of the room were impressive enough, but it was what the room held that made it hard for Emma to even get out words of thanks; she was so overwhelmed. It had been outfitted as a painting studio, all of her things moved, but also added to.

Everything she could imagine needing to paint, not just her commissions, but multiple easels and a full set of watercolors, as well as acrylics and oils with the top-of-the-line brushes to go with each. A lot of artists stuck to one medium, but she'd always been happiest when she could flit back and forth between these three.

She looked at Kon. "You remembered."

"I remember everything about you," he promised her. "You said that your ideal studio would have the space for all your supplies and you would not have to pack up one medium to start a project with another."

It had been her dream, but one she'd never realized. She'd felt lucky to have room for any kind of studio in her and Mickey's little house. Being able to keep art in her life at all had been a luxury, but necessary for her sense of well-being. She'd stuck to watercolors for her commissions and had stifled every desire to create with something else.

"Look, Mom, see all the windows?" Mickey spread his arms expansively.

Emma grinned. "I do. They're wonderful." She

opened her arms and got a big hug from her son. "You're wonderful. Thank you, Mickey."

"And Dad. It was his idea, but he wanted my help. He took me shopping."

That was some commitment to her happiness right there. Mickey was not the greatest shopper. He got bored when he wasn't moving.

Emma smiled at Kon. "Thank you. Really. This is amazing."

"Do I get a hug too?" he asked, a devilish glint in his eyes.

"You've gotta give Dad a hug too," Mickey demanded.

Emma gave her son a gently reproving look. "Hugs are always voluntary, you know that, Mickey."

"Right. Because we set our body boundaries," he parroted what she'd told him a hundred times and she was sure his preschool staff had as well. "But Mom, he tried real hard to make you happy."

Kon opened his arms, his expression quizzical and just a little bit challenging. It was the challenge that did it. Her back up, Emma found herself moving across the tile floor to him with determined movements.

She meant to give him a distance hug. Nothing too personal. Perfunctory. Only, her body leaned into his like it had been programmed to his touch. Maybe it had.

He had been her first and only real lover.

The last man she'd let into her personal space without limits. Somehow she let herself relax into his body, her arms going around him in anything but a *perfunctory* manner.

"Thank you," she whispered huskily into his chest.

Kon's arms wrapped tightly around her, pulling her even closer. "My pleasure."

That short, throwaway phrase held so much meaning beyond *you're welcome*. The way he held her, the unmistakable proof that this hug was having the same physical effect on him that it was her... It all said this moment really was *his* pleasure.

But it was hers too and that scared the life out of her. Even so, she stayed where she was.

Everything she'd told herself about getting over him was suddenly shown for the lies they had been.

Emma inhaled and his scent washed over her with all the sense memories it could invoke. Lazy Sunday mornings spent in bed, touching, laughing...talking. Nights of passion that left her replete and certain of her place in the world. Peaceful moments cuddling on the couch, watching his sports on the television, while she read a book.

For a moment she was back in that place, in love, certain she was cared for, the future nebulous but shiny.

"That's a good hug." Mickey's voice jarred, bringing Emma back to the present with a thump. "She can hug you like that cuz you're my dad. We're family."

Emma shoved against Kon, jumping back and nearly tripping over her own feet to put distance between them. Only then did she notice the pained look on his face. Her gaze skimmed his body and guilt assailed her. She quickly stepped between him and their son's line of sight.

The look of gratitude Kon shot her did a number on her heart.

"Right, Mom?" Mickey asked, his little face showing tension she hadn't noticed at first.

"Um…" Oh, man, what was she supposed to say?

I just hugged the stuffing out of your father because I forgot where I was, when I was and how much this man hurt me once upon a time.

Not. Going. To. Happen.

"*Da*, Mishka, I *am* your dad and we *are* a family." Kon, in his typical arrogant, I-know-what's-best fashion, had decided to answer.

The fact he stayed where he was, which showed he wasn't able to get over his reaction to holding her that easily, gave her some satisfaction though.

"Mom?" Mickey wanted full-on assurance.

And Emma did what she was always did when her son needed anything it was in her power to provide. She gave it. "Yes, sweetheart, we are a family. I can hug your dad when I need to."

"And he can hug you, right, Mom?"

If Emma had a potty mouth it would have gotten a workout right then, if only inside her own mind. Wrapped neatly and tied with a bow by her own son.

"I'm sure he'd rather hug you than me," Emma said evasively.

"I don't think so, Mom." Mickey looked at Kon. "You like hugging Mom, huh? You looked really happy hugging her."

"I enjoy hugging you both very much," Kon said smoothly, making no effort to dissuade their son from his family-hugging agenda.

The rat.

"Because we're a family." Mickey's happiness with that truth was as obvious as a bright yellow swath down the middle of a desert watercolor.

Bright and out of place it might be in the desert of

her life, Emma couldn't bring herself to dampen even the edges of her son's joy.

"Yes," Emma affirmed.

Mickey's smile let Emma know she'd made the right choice, but his father's smile worried her more than a little.

As the day wore on, it became clear that Mickey had appointed himself the role of matchmaker. Making sure that if they sat together, she and Kon were side by side. Talking about the future all bright and shiny as a family *all together*. Talking his dad up to Emma with a canny understanding that she was the one with reservations.

All of it so very clearly revealing Mickey's plans of seeing his parents reunited.

If Emma thought Kon had put him up to his shenanigans, she would be furious. But she didn't.

Mickey had been up-front and loud about his desire for family that was more than just him and Emma since meeting his father. He adored Kon and thrived under his father's affection and presence.

Emma realized that her own need to protect her heart had taken a toll on her son's sense of security. He'd had only one adult in his life he knew he could absolutely rely on.

Her highly intelligent but equally sensitive son had felt the lack keenly.

That night as she and Kon tucked Mickey in, he said, "Now there's someone to take care of you, Mom." He smiled up at his father with trust she was used to seeing doled out only in *her* direction. "You'll always watch out for us, right, Dad?"

"*Da.* I promise you with all that I am." Kon's voice rang with the sincerity and permanence of a vow.

Hearing her son use that comfort-seeking phrase toward someone else went through Emma with a painful jolt.

It was hard to relinquish her spot as his only mainstay, but even more painful was the realization Mickey had needed to know she had backup. And she'd never given him that.

Fighting emotions she could not cope with right then, she kissed her son good-night and told him she loved him.

"Love you too, Mom. Love you, Dad."

"I love you too, Mishka," Kon promised as he tucked the blankets just a little tighter around him. Then he leaned down and kissed Mickey's forehead before standing. "See you in the morning."

"Or in the night if I have a bad dream, right?"

"Absolutely. Your mom and I are just across the hall." He made it sound like they were sharing a room, which they were not, but it was part of that illusion they both seemed intent on building around her.

A full-on family with all the connections.

Mickey nodded sleepily and turned to his side, contentment coming off him in waves.

Emma stumbled from his room, headed for her own.

"Emma."

She stopped at Kon's voice, but did not turn around. "What?"

"I thought we could spend some time together."

"Not tonight." Her voice caught and she knew the tears she was fighting were too close to the surface.

"Emma, what is the matter? It was a good day, was it not?" Kon's hand landed on her shoulder.

Emma shuddered, that small connection more than her starving senses could handle.

He turned her, oh, so gently, his expression perplexed. "What is it, Emma *moi*?"

"You used to call me that all the time. But I'm not yours anymore, Kon."

"I think you have always been mine. And I have always been yours." He said it like he really believed his own words.

Only they could not be true.

She laughed, the sound too close to a sob for comfort. "Your legion of lovers would say otherwise."

"No legion and not one of them was a *lover*. I had sex partners and if could change that now, I would." His brown eyes were dark with some kind of intense emotion.

Maybe he did regret sleeping with other women, though she didn't know why he should. They hadn't been together. There had been no promises between them, not after Kon had evicted Emma from his life.

"Do you think it matters that you didn't give them your heart?" He'd said that like it made *all* the difference, but it didn't make *any* difference. Not to her. "You never gave me that either."

The only thing that made her special in his life was that she'd given birth to his son. Emma needed to remember that, or she was going to get her heart shattered all over again.

"I think the only thing that matters is what happens now. We cannot change the past, no matter how much we may wish we could."

She had no trouble believing her Prince genuinely wished things had gone differently. He already loved Mickey and Kon had missed out on almost five years of his life.

"You would have loved being a dad from day one, even I can see that," Emma had no problem acknowledging.

"You and Mishka are the only ones who matter."

But Kon was wrong about that. "I should have given him more family."

"What?" he asked, sounding genuinely shocked. "Emma, you are an amazing mom."

"I let my own insecurities stop me from providing my son with what he needed," she admitted with shame. "That's not amazing. That's cowardly."

"No." Kon jerked his head in a negative motion, his expression filled with denial. "If there is a woman who is less a coward, I do not know her."

The tears fell then. Because Emma knew he was wrong. Unable to speak, she just shook her head.

Kon made a sound like his patient understanding had lost the fight with his need to act, and then he was picking her up.

She gasped her shock, but it came out choked with her tears.

His expression grim, Kon asked, "Your room, or mine?"

Even if she knew why he was asking, she couldn't have answered. Emma was too busy having a meltdown. She never cried. Never. She meditated. She did yoga. Emma did not lose it, emotionally, but right now? She was definitely losing it.

And instead of running in the other direction like

a smart man would have, Kon was throwing himself into it like he could stand between her and her own emotional pain.

"Mine, then," he said, decisively. "It has been sound-proofed. Mishka will not hear you crying."

Emma didn't ask why the master bedroom was soundproofed, only grateful that her son would not be woken by the sobs she didn't seem able to stifle.

Kon carried her into his room toward a butter yellow leather sofa near the tall windows. They overlooked the gorgeous pool area the three of them had spent time in after lunch. She'd been laughing and full of a sense of freedom, not being Mickey's only caretaker then, not the blubbering mess she was now.

Emma wouldn't have blamed him if he dumped her on the sofa and retreated, but Kon sat down without letting her go, settling Emma in his lap.

And she let him.

His arms were steady bands around her, his solid chest right there for her to rest her head against. "Tell me what is going through your mind to upset you so much," he insisted.

"Don't you see?" she implored him. "I was afraid to let anyone in and because of that, Mickey didn't have the people in his life he needed."

"I don't understand." Kon's brows drew together in a frown of confusion.

"He had no grandparents, no aunts and uncles."

Kon's gorgeous features were cast with guilt, show-ing just who he thought was at fault. *Him*. "But that was not your fault."

But it wasn't entirely his either. Emma had her own burden of guilt she was just coming face-to-face with. "I could have built a family for him. Mrs. Jensen wanted to be my friend but I wouldn't even call her by her first name. It was Claire. I never used it. Not once. She needed a friend too."

But Emma had been too raw with loss to make friends with her employer. Later, she'd built walls around her heart she hadn't even realized were there.

"Because the people you had trusted with your heart crushed it." Kon's expression was as if light had dawned over the horizon to illuminate and turn dark, impenetrable shapes into something recognizable. "Your parents, me… We let you down so badly you didn't trust anyone else."

"And hurt my son in the process." She gulped in air, trying to control the tears. "I thought I'd got it together. That I hadn't let myself become that cynical, broken soul. But all the time I was so proud of my inner peace, I *was* that woman and I kept everyone who could have given Mickey a sense of security at a distance."

"Mishka had you. He was safe. He was loved."

"But he was worried!" She pressed her fist against Kon's chest. "I should have dated Mr. Leeds. Mickey adores him."

"No, he's not the right man for you," Kon slotted in with speed. "He's too young for you. You have nothing in common with him."

"He's closer in age to me than you are." She had no idea if she had anything in common with the preschool teacher, or not. Emma hadn't allowed him to get close enough to find out. Even as a friend.

"Mishka has grandparents, an aunt, two uncles. We will bring them all into his life. I promise you."

"But he should have had other people all along."

"Stop this. Emma, your tears…no." Kon sounded nearly panicked. "You will stop crying and worrying about the past. Mishka is a well-adjusted, happy child. Stop beating yourself up."

She'd never heard him less than fully confident. Emma would have laughed at him instructing her to stop crying if she could have.

He was so arrogant and so very clearly out of his depth right then.

"But look how he is looking to you for reassurance now." It shamed her to admit, but that still hurt.

"Because you have allowed it. Your love for our son has enabled you to see beyond my monumental mistakes and allow me into his life. *You* gave him a father and now he has both of us to give him security, but only because your generous heart made that possible."

Konstantin did not know if he was saying the right things. He only knew he could not stand to see his Emma hurting like this.

He wasn't such an oblivious fool that he did not see how hard it was for her to share their son with him. Emma and Mikhail had been their own little family since his birth. Konstantin fully expected his son to go through some adjustments learning to share his mom's attention and affection as well.

But Konstantin was up to the task.

He was in regular contact with not only his family, but also Mikhail's counselor, seeking advice. Only no wise words could prepare him for this moment when the woman he wanted to be his wife cried in his arms because she thought she hadn't been a good enough single mom.

"You have been strong when Mishka needed strength. You gave him tenderness when he needed it. He lacked for nothing, do you hear me?" Konstantin willed her to believe him.

A watery laugh erupted from her and she gave him a wry look, no less effective for the tears standing in her beautiful blue eyes. "Just because you say it doesn't make it so."

"I am sure it does. I am a prince, if you did not know it."

Another choky laugh sounded. "I know it."

He considered those two moments of shaky laughter some of his best work.

Her fingers kneaded his chest in what he was sure was unconscious movement without any of the sexual intentions his body was reading into the action.

No thoughts of football stats or spreadsheet formulas could cool the ardor growing in Konstantin's body. He had craved this woman since the moment she walked out of his life. That it had been at his insistence did not matter.

No woman he had been with since had ever fulfilled that craving, or made him miss Emma any less.

She shifted in his lap and then stilled. "Kon?"

She could not know how much pleasure he derived by her calling him Kon like she used to. He wasn't about to point it out either.

Contrary woman that she was, she would probably make herself stop doing it.

"Ignore it. I cannot control my body's base reaction to you, but that does not mean I have to act on it." He was no hormonal adolescent.

Tension that had nothing to do with Emma's meltdown thrummed between them. Heated sexual desire charged the air around them so much he would not have been surprised to see actual sparks.

"That's not what you used to say." Her beautiful blue eyes were filled with feminine mystery.

Which only added to the ardent need growing in him to have her back in his bed, but even more important, she was no longer crying.

"I was an ass, pressing you into a physical relationship you weren't ready for. I'm sorry." It was an apology long overdue.

"No apology needed. For that anyway. Make no mistake, I was ready for it." She pressed her fingertip to his lips when he went to interrupt. "Listen, Kon, I may not have been ready for what came after, but I wanted you every bit as much as you wanted me."

"I knew what was coming, but you did not."

"The breakup, you mean?"

"Yes. You were right, I should have reminded you that what we had was not permanent." He'd convinced himself that telling her that one time was enough.

It had not been. Full. Stop.

"Maybe part of you wished it could be."

"Maybe. I did not allow myself to entertain thoughts in that direction, but nor did I dwell on the inevitable end."

She pushed against his chest and as much as he hated to, Konstantin had to let her get up. He was pleasantly surprised when she moved only as far as the seat beside him on the sofa.

"You said that you finally reneged on the contract when Princess Nataliya embarrassed you in the media."

This was not something Konstantin wanted to talk

about, but with Emma, he found himself willing to do what was not comfortable for him. In many ways.

"Yes, I did." His brother had spun it for the media like Nikolai had swooped in and stolen Nataliya from under Konstantin's nose.

But the truth was that Konstantin had played right into his sister-in-law's hands and rejected her as a potential wife in front of their two families, all but negating the contract.

"It's hard to accept that you were willing to break the contract you held as sacrosanct for the sake of your pride, but hadn't been willing to do it so we could stay together."

"I did not see it that way." And would never have suspected she did.

Her mind was still a big mystery to him in so many ways and yet he felt like he knew her better than anyone else in his life and that she knew him more deeply than even his own family.

"How else could you see it?" she asked, like she really wanted him to answer. Like Emma, the amazing woman she was, was *willing* to listen.

"When we were together, I never even let myself consider breaking the contract and trying to build a future with you."

"I'm not exactly princess material."

"Technically as my wife, you would have the title of duchess until Nikolai decreed otherwise, but Emma, it had nothing to do with that."

"What, then?"

"I'd made a promise. I had to keep it."

"You broke it later."

"I had changed, my perception of what I owed my family had changed."

"What changed it?" Emma's blue gaze demanded full honesty.

Konstantin could not deny her that, even if telling her things he'd never shared with anyone else left him feeling exposed. "At first, I thought it was losing my friend. Tiana was so young when she died, and her death made me reexamine my own life."

"You said you went looking for me then," Emma said, sounding thoughtful.

"I did, but you were gone and I was still stuck in the groove of believing that contract dictated my ultimate future."

"But something changed."

"Time changed me. Having sex with women that were not you changed me." This was the hardest thing to admit. It showed her how much he needed her, and Konstantin did not like needing anyone. "It was empty and one day I had the lowering realization that was what marriage to Nataliya was going to be like. I'd had perfection and knew what it felt like to share something more than empty, fleeting pleasure with a woman."

Emma gasped as if his words had shocked her to the core. "You didn't see our time together that way."

"I assure you, I did."

"So, you're trying to tell me that having sex with other women made you realize that what we'd had was special."

Konstantin felt heat climb his neck. "Yes."

"But while we were together you didn't think it was so special." She left unsaid that if he had, he would not have broken up with her.

"Please try to understand. I was not raised to consider my *feelings*, my *emotions* as any kind of valid basis for making choices. Our parents were loving toward us, but if they loved each other, I never knew it. They loved Mirrus and its people. Their actions were driven by that love and duty."

"Duty they taught you to revere."

"Yes." Could she understand?

A woman raised to honor her parents, but without the weight of royal duty he had known from his first memory.

"I can't say that makes the past okay, but I think I'm starting to understand what drove your actions then and now."

That was something. "Thank you."

"For what?"

"For listening. For trying to understand a perspective very different from your own. We should all aspire to be so open to those we don't understand."

"That's a great attitude even if you are kind of overblowing my virtues."

She was so humble, maybe too humble. "Not at all. I have it on the best authority, our son's if you are wondering, that you are *the best*."

"And I thought it was only your praises he was singing to me."

"Oh, no. That child has plans and I'm not sure either of us is going to be able to stand against them."

"According to you, you don't want to."

"True." And maybe she didn't want to so much either any longer.

Emma's smile went straight to his groin.

He offered a promise that he thought she might need, and even if she didn't, he needed to give.

"I don't know if you will ever forgive me those other women, but I promise you that if you marry me, there will never be another." Even if Emma never agreed to marry him, Konstantin doubted he could ever settle for empty sex again.

"You think I need to forgive you for sleeping around *after* we broke up?" she asked.

"Yes." Emma might not realize it, but Konstantin was sure of it.

She was his. He was hers. Even if they had not been together. He had betrayed that in an attempt to prove that he *didn't* need her and had only succeeded in proving to himself that no other woman could ever replace her in his life.

Even if he'd followed through on that damn contract.

"If Nataliya and I had actually made it to the wedding, I would have left her waiting at the altar. And I'm not proud of that," he admitted.

But even now, even after everything, he could tell Emma things he would never admit to another living soul.

"You wouldn't have," Emma said, sounding very sure.

"I would. I could never have spoken the vows to her. They would have been a lie."

"That sounds an awful lot like you loved me."

Konstantin felt those words like an ice pick to his soul. "Love? No. Emma, I know you think you need me to love you to marry me, but consider, I am offering a companionship that few ever experience, sexual compatibility that is *very* special and fidelity in both body and mind."

"But not love?" she sounded more musing than upset by that.

"I don't think I'm capable of romantic love. I'm just not wired that way," he admitted, hoping his honesty wasn't scuppering his efforts at courtship.

Courtship. Konstantin let out a humorless laugh. He now understood what that word meant. And it wasn't just sending a bunch of meaningless gifts to a woman.

It was *working* to show her that their lives would be better joined than apart.

"What is funny?" she asked, her voice gentle, her lovely features open in a way they had not been since he ran into her in that bank.

"I finally realized what it means to court a woman."

"Oh, and what does it mean?"

"You are going to find out," he promised.

His brother wasn't the only son of the Royal House of Merikov that knew how to court a woman.

"If my new art studio and the effort you make with our son is any indication, I'm going to enjoy it very much."

Konstantin suddenly realized that this woman deserved every bit of the courtship he had not given her before. When he hadn't been able to see her as anything but a temporary lover.

It would be no platonic courtship though. He would be a fool to give up the one area he'd always gotten right with her.

And Konstantin's father hadn't raised any fools.

Emma wasn't sure what that expression on Kon's face meant, but it intrigued her and sent a frisson of feminine awareness through her.

His gaze locked with hers, Kon pulled her hand to his lips and kissed her palm, flicking his tongue out to tease.

Need kindled by Emma's first sight of him at the bank whooshed into a flash fire. An all-over body shudder sent that heat spiking through her every capillary. Emma's nipples peaked into aching rigidity just that fast, her sex contracted with need, her lips parted ready for his kiss, her eyes slid shut as decadent anticipation rolled over her.

All from that single sensual caress of his tongue against her palm.

Memories of him turning her hands into erogenous zones, of tasting her entire body with that clever tongue, inundated her so that it was hard to separate the past from the present. Her body was starved for his touch, but she hadn't known it.

She knew it now.

Could not miss how everything in her strained for his touch.

His big body moved, Emma's heightened awareness telling her he was closer than he had been. Warm air puffed over her lips as he asked, "May I kiss you?"

"Yes." Her brain screamed caution; her body wasn't listening.

The kiss, when it came, was electrifying, everything she remembered and more somehow. His lips moved gently over hers at first, like he was relearning the taste and texture of her lips.

She responded in kind, molding her mouth to his. Emotions she thought long buried if not obliterated entirely erupted inside her, causing a maelstrom of feelings she no longer had a compass to navigate.

She hadn't been kissed like this in more than five
years, but it *had* been years and what had once been oh,
so natural between them was now something different.

Something intense and dangerous.

She no longer trusted this man with her heart, but
her body craved him so badly she felt she'd fly apart
if they didn't keep kissing.

Sensation poured through Emma, strong and ur-
gent, setting every single nerve ending alight with anticipation.

With need.

With longing.

A longing that was familiar from a very different
setting.

How many nights had she lain awake, aching for
this man after he dumped her?

Pregnancy had sent her hormones into overdrive,
intensifying every single unrequited emotion and un-
fulfilled desire.

Those memories filled her with a kind of dread even
as her body strained toward his.

Emma pulled away from the kiss, panting.

CHAPTER EIGHT

"WHAT?" KON ASKED, his pupils blown with pleasure. "What is it? I locked the door. So Mickey wouldn't just walk in on you crying," he hurriedly clarified.

Emma's brain wasn't working at its normal speed. It took her a moment to realize he thought she might believe he'd planned this.

The kiss. A seduction.

Honestly? Maybe he had. Maybe he hadn't.

Right now it wasn't his plans that had her in knots. It was her memories. Her fears.

She gulped in a breath. "Give me a second. I need…"

"What do you need?" he asked when she didn't finish her thought.

Distance. Control. A steel case for her heart.

Something to protect her emotions.

When they'd been together before, Emma had dived headlong into the sensual tsunami that was their lovemaking.

She'd let her heart rule her head. Her libido had fed her heart's desires, but that had led to an emotional devastation and loss she never wanted to experience again.

She couldn't afford to let herself drown in sensation like this.

"What?" Kon repeated. "What is it?"

"I just need to catch my breath." Emma pulled in air and released it, trying to bring her desire under some kind of control.

"Let's both get breathless," he invited, his dark eyes glowing with masculine need. "I want to give you more pleasure than you've ever known."

Emma's thighs pressed together convulsively, her entire body quivering with anticipation at that promise.

She had no doubt he would keep it.

But her brain, the atavistic part that warned her of dangerous driving conditions and questionable sur- roundings, sent out a warning claxon.

"What happens after the pleasure?" she asked, baldly.

"Whatever you want to."

"But…" Her wants had played no role in what hap- pened the last time.

"Emma, this *is* a courtship. Make no mistake, my end game is marriage, but I need you as I have never needed another woman. I believe you need me too."

"Sexually," she clarified, knowing he did not need her heart like she'd needed his at one time.

"To start," he said and then kissed her softly, almost tentatively. "Yes?"

In a moment of perfect clarity, Emma realized this was the direction they'd been headed ever since his first clumsy, unromantic proposal.

He was looking at a long-term future for them. Something that had never been on the table before.

It was now.

It was not love. It was not even romance.

It was mutual need. Mutual desire. It was an acknowledgment that she was special in his life and her admitting, if only to herself, that he was still someone she wanted in hers.

"Yes," she whispered against his lips and then Emma deepened the kiss on her own.

He tasted so good, his lips moved so perfectly against her own, his tongue teasing hers into responding.

But she didn't want only to respond. She wanted to make him as hot for her as she was for him.

If she was going to do this, Emma was going to get maximum pleasure from it.

She climbed into Kon's lap, his hard thighs under hers driving her ardor higher. They both started shedding clothes, breaking their kiss only to get her top off, and then his shirt.

Buttons popped, scattering with little tings across the floor, and neither of them cared.

They touched and squirmed and managed to divest themselves and each other of every stitch of clothing, all the while caressing each other like two desperate teenagers.

Kon's usual finesse was entirely missing, but then Emma wasn't any better. She wanted to feel every change five years had wrought on his body. The way his fingertips mapped her stomach, her thighs, her shoulders, everything in between said Kon wanted the same thing.

Emma rubbed the apex of her thighs against his erection, pleasuring them both.

Kon's big body shuddered, his mouth breaking from hers to trail biting kisses down her neck. "Yes, Emma, that's right, *solnyshko*."

The familiar endearment was like another touch right to the core of her. He used to call her his *little sunshine* because he said she brought light into his life.

Had he missed that light all this time?

He clasped her hips, but let her set the pace and ferocity of their bodies' movement together.

Emma remembered *this*.

Kon might be a prince and a totally take-charge kind of guy, but he'd never needed to completely control their lovemaking. He always encouraged Emma to seek her own pleasure and seemed to derive his own from it. In a very big way.

He thrust up, meeting her body with his own, increasing the pressure of his sex against her clitoris and sending ecstasy arcing through her.

"Touch me," Emma demanded, thrusting her breasts against his hard chest.

Kon muttered something in Russian against her ear, the puffs of air sending shivers rolling through her. It must not have been a denial because his big hands shifted to cup her curves, thumbs brushing over already stiff and sensitive peaks.

The caresses went straight to her core and Emma moaned, pleasure building inside her along with a need to be filled that would not be denied.

They kissed again, Emma matching Kon touch for touch, their bodies moving in an increasingly frantic rhythm.

One of Kon's hands moved down over her backside, sliding down until his fingertip dipped inside her most intimate flesh. She was wet and swollen and he moved easily inside her despite the years since she had been this close to another person.

He added another finger almost immediately, pressing in and out of her body, making love to her with his hand even as she craved the ultimate connection.

Her climax hit her out of nowhere, rolling over her body with so much intensity she screamed against his lips and then tried to hold back further cries.

"Give me all your sounds."

"But Mickey—"

"Can hear nothing."

Emma rubbed herself against Kon, enjoying the aftershocks of pleasure and making no further effort to stifle her cries.

Despite the powerful orgasm and its aftershocks, Emma never went limp in satiation.

"The soundproofing. That's why," she gasped against him, shuddering with prolonged pleasure.

"Yes." He arched up against her and groaned. "Also because I believe there should always be a safe room to discuss things that small ears cannot accidentally overhear."

"You were very sure of yourself."

"I had hope, Emma. Hope and need that only you can meet." The way he moved against her so frantically gave credence to his claim.

"Is this part of the courtship?" she asked breathlessly.

He went very still and very serious, his chocolate gaze locking on hers. "Between us how can it not be?"

Emma had no answer as Kon claimed her mouth again. His lips were so very familiar and yet not.

Her body just craved more after such a long drought of this type of pleasure. Emma shifted and Kon seemed to know what she wanted because he slid his fingers out of her to grab his own sex and hold it in position for her.

She slid down, taking his sex into her waiting channel, reveling in every millimeter of stretch to tender tissues. Emma had always loved the feel of Kon inside her and that had not diminished in the years apart.

She rocked her hips until he filled her completely, pressing against her cervix and sending shards of sharp pleasure through her.

Kon's hand pressed on her backside, encouraging her to move.

Emma was only too happy to oblige, lifting her hips and then lowering them down, pleasuring them both.

Kon broke their kiss, gasping. "Birth control." His jaw was so taut, he looked in pain. "I need a condom," he gritted out.

Emma stilled, need and common sense at war in her body.

It could be too late already, they both knew that. She was not on any form of birth control. There had been no call for it since their breakup.

Using every nanometer of her self-control, Emma remained motionless and met Kon's eyes.

His expression was intense and filled with heated desire. "I want more children with you, *solnyshko*, but that will be a decision we make together, and not when we need each other so badly we are both shaking with it."

She nodded, unutterably touched by his care for her. He'd never taken risks with her body. She'd gotten

pregnant with Mickey when her birth control failed,
not because either of them had dismissed the need
for it.

Still so turned on she felt on the verge of a second
climax, Emma went to move off Konstantin.

However, he stood up before she could do so, one
arm firmly under her bottom and the other wrapped
around her back, keeping their bodies connected in the
most intimate way.

He carried her to the bed and laid her down, with-
drawing from her body only then, and eliciting a whim-
per of need from her.

"You are so beautiful, Emma." Kon's expression
was filled with something she could not read, but the
admiration was genuine and easy to see. *"Krasavitsa."*

She felt a purely feminine smile come over her features. "I'm glad you still find me attractive. Giving
birth to Mickey changed my body."

"You are everything that turns me on," he said in
a guttural tone, all smooth prince charm in abeyance.
"All the more so because of those changes that testify
to you giving birth to my child."

Those words fell like sweet water on the parched
recesses of her heart. Kon wasn't, and had never been,
looking for plastic perfection.

He wanted a real woman. He wanted *her*.

"You're physically it for me too, Kon." The only man
who had ever been worth lowering her defenses for.

The first time had ended in heartache, but this time
she wasn't trusting blindly and he was offering permanence even when she said she didn't want it.

He leaned down to grab a condom from his bedside

table. He fumbled and swore when it slipped from his hand and went sailing when he tried to tear it open.

This sign that he was as lost to need as she was only sent Emma's desire skyrocketing even as she smiled at him. "Having trouble there, stud?"

He growled. Like some big jungle cat. He grabbed another one, tearing it open with his teeth this time and then rolling it on with a look of pained ecstasy that sent pleasure jolting through her.

Kon came down over her, but even as he kissed her, he rolled them so she was on top again.

She leaned up, sitting on top of him, sliding her body so they were once again angled for perfect penetration. There was no buildup this time; she took him inside her in one downward thrust.

They both groaned and she started moving, riding him with absolute intent.

There would be no more interruptions. For this moment he was entirely hers and she held nothing back as she brought them closer and closer to orgasm.

He praised her, his hands running over her body in knowing caresses, giving pleasure and driving them both higher and higher.

He came first this time, his shout loud and all primal male.

She grabbed one of his hands, pressing it against her mound and he touched her just like she needed, bringing her over the precipice. Her entire body convulsed, her inner walls contracting around him, the pleasure exploding through her like a hurricane wave crashing over the shore.

She collapsed down on top of him and he hugged her to him like he couldn't let her go.

Emma patted his chest with a desultory movement. "That's every bit as good as it ever was."

"Better." Kon hugged her tighter. "Better."

It had been amazing, but better? "Why better?"

"Because for the first time I made love to you without knowing in the back of my mind there was a time coming when I had to let you go."

Sometimes…he said stuff that made her think he *did* love her. Like the way he'd described how he felt about her earlier. And now, talking like his worry that he was going to lose her eventually had always colored their time before.

In a bad way, not an inevitable-change way.

Emma wanted to believe that Kon just didn't understand his own feelings, but she'd made the mistake of believing his unstated feelings were something they were not before.

She would never allow herself such naive optimism again.

He'd hurt her too badly. Her son had been hurt too badly for her to delude herself.

Even so, there could be no denying that Kon wanted a future with her.

Emma just didn't know if she could trust that future.

And she wasn't taking his word for it that his royal family supported his marrying her without meeting them first.

Emma went to shift, but Kon's arms tightened around her.

"Let me go, stud. You've got to take care of the condom," she reminded him.

They'd already taken a big enough risk.

He grunted agreement and let her move off him

then, before rolling off the bed to do what he had to. He was back moments later, pulling her into his arms.

"I'm not sleeping here, Kon."

"Why not?" he asked, sounding *hurt*?

Emma steeled herself against giving in. "Mickey doesn't need to find us in the same bed."

"He wants us to be a family."

"We are a family. You said it before, whether we marry or don't marry, we will always be connected through Mickey."

"I love my son, but he is not the only connection I want to have with you, Emma."

"I believe you."

"You do?"

"Yes, but…"

"But? How did I know there had to be a *but*?"

Emma couldn't help smiling. "Because you know me."

Kon's smile was sensual as well as amused. "I do know you, so tell me about this *but*."

"I want to go to Mirrus." His family had all signed the custody agreement. Even so, it was a huge step of trust for her to take, but Emma couldn't figure out how to find out what she needed to without meeting a bunch of royals.

"I thought we were going to Seattle from here?" he asked, his dark brows drawn together in question.

"I want to go to Mirrus first."

"Why?" Kon didn't sound worried, just curious.

"I want to meet your family."

"You want to know they support us being together like I told you."

"I never said you were stupid," she commented, tongue in cheek.

But Kon frowned. "I bet you did, after I dumped you and you were pregnant with Mishka and could not contact me to tell me about our son. I bet you thought I was stupid then."

"I thought you were lots of things, but most of them were wrong, so let's not dwell on that time."

"So, Mirrus?"

"Yes. I want to see how your family reacts to Mickey." How they reacted to her as Mickey's mother.

"My father will be thrilled. He's threatened to come to New Mexico more than once. He wants to meet his grandson badly."

"Threatened?" She latched onto that word quickly.

"For me having him show up while I am doing my best to court you and build a relationship with my son is a threat."

"I see."

"He wants to meet you as well. He wants to apologize."

"For what?"

"For pushing me into breaking up with you."

"He did?" That did not sound good.

"He didn't know he was doing it. He was upset I had not fulfilled the contract yet and put me on some pretty spectacular guilt trips until I agreed to start things in motion with Nataliya."

"Only you had to break up with me first."

Which spoke well of Kon's personal integrity.

"Yes."

"You didn't get together with Nataliya though."

"I needed time to get over us."

"I bet that didn't make your dad happy."

"Considering he had no idea why I was dragging my feet? No. He was very angry with me."

"And then Queen Tiana died."

"And I was off the hook." At least during the period of formal mourning.

Even an announcement of engagement would have been considered in poor taste during that time. Not to mention, it would have been unkind to flaunt the idea of marriage in front of his brother who had just lost a wife.

That his father had not continued to push the issue after that time was up was something he'd always been grateful for and hadn't questioned too closely.

"But not entirely."

"No." Kon shrugged. "Though I put off fulfilling the contract as long as I could."

"Why?" Emma didn't believe Kon had been holding out for getting back together with her.

"Nataliya had a thing for my brother. She always felt more like my sister than my potential bride."

"But you did court her."

It was Kon's turn to grimace. "I had my staff send her gifts and flowers. I never even called her."

"Not much of a courtship."

"It was a business deal." He shrugged. "Not a romance."

"Are we a romance?" He had said he wanted to court her.

"We belong to each other. I am the best man for you. You are the ideal woman for me. Courting you is only natural."

Typical Kon, avoid a *yes or no* answer if it wasn't

what he thought she wanted to hear. But his answer wasn't a bad one regardless.

"Hmm…" Emma didn't quite know what to say to that.

He was talking like his feelings for her were something deeper again, but Kon had been pretty clear that he didn't consider himself capable of romantic love.

"When do you want to go to Mirrus?" Kon asked her.

"Mickey graduates from preschool in two weeks. We can plan to fly out any time after that, but do you have business in Seattle you have to attend to?"

"I can work from Mirrus as well as Seattle, if not as efficiently."

"Okay."

"We will fly out the day after Mishka's graduation. Is he really going to wear a graduation gown?"

"Yes. I ordered it months ago. It's pretty adorable. We went to last year's graduation so he could watch his friends. I've rarely seen anything as cute."

"Do many preschools do this?"

"All the ones I know of do it now." All the ones she'd researched for both her charges when she'd been a nanny and those schools she'd looked into for Mickey.

"That is sweet."

"Mickey's really excited about it."

"I know."

Emma smiled. They'd both heard how excited their son was about the ceremony. Even the prospect of leaving his beloved teacher behind wasn't dimming his enthusiasm.

But then he had a father now, someone who took precedence over Mr. Leeds.

"I need to get to my own bed. Thank you for letting me cry all over you."

"Thank you for showing me the honor of trusting me with your tears."

Emma wasn't sure if she'd trusted him so much as hit her limit and he'd been there for the fallout. She didn't disillusion him, however. Kon seemed too happy to think she'd cried on him on purpose.

She went to slide from the bed, but Kon was there.

He kissed her lips until she was panting and then moved down to that spot behind her ear. "We're not done, I don't think."

And they weren't. They made love again, and this time he set the pace, seemingly determined to wring every last ounce of pleasure from Emma's body.

It was all she could do not to fall into a comatose sleep after, but Emma made it back to her own room and her own bed, only to immediately miss Kon and his warmth.

But their son didn't need to get any more ideas than he already had about them, she reminded herself.

Sleep was a long time coming.

The next two weeks flew by, Kon working a little more than he had when he'd stayed at her house, Emma finishing up her notice and then overseeing the movers Kon had hired to pack her and Mickey's things to ship to Seattle.

They kept some favorite toys and books, and, of course, clothes for the remainder of their time in Santa Fe and for use on their trip to Mirrus.

Not as many clothes as she'd planned because Kon insisted on buying both her and Mickey wardrobes more appropriate for the colder climate of Mirrus. It might be summer, but he informed them both they would need warmer clothes.

Kon even ordered Mickey two suits tailored to fit their son perfectly even though he would probably grow out of them in a matter of months.

"Why does Mickey need suits?" Emma asked in bemusement as her son showed as much excitement over the formalwear as he had the new game system Kon had purchased.

"He'll wear one to graduation."

"Yes, and?"

"I'll be like Dad!" Mickey said excitedly. "I'll look so fly for my graduation and to meet the King."

"Fly?" Emma asked.

"Another word we can probably thank Mr. Leeds for."

"Oh." Her son was growing so fast and changing even faster. "Mickey, you *want* to wear suits?"

"I'm an earl, Mom. I need to look like Dad."

Emma held back her grimace at the noble title. Mickey said it the same way he announced he was four years and three-quarters. With pride and practicality.

It just was.

Something else that just was? The incredible sexual intimacy between Kon and Emma. He might be working more now, but he'd still managed to take advantage of time alone in the house without Mickey while their son was at preschool on several occasions.

And every night, Kon invited her into his bed after they put their son in his own.

Sometimes those invitations took the form of words. Sometimes, Kon just picked Emma up and carried her into the giant master bedroom.

He always asked before the first kiss. He always wore a condom and she always climaxed at least twice.

The pleasure should have just been physical, but every time they made love, Emma's emotions came closer and closer to the surface.

CHAPTER NINE

IF EMMA HAD thought that tailored suits for their son, and the other myriad clothes Kon had insisted on buying for Mickey, were over the top, her Prince's plans for expanding Emma's wardrobe blew her away.

He had representatives from three top designers bring a selection of casual to formalwear in the colors she'd learned to love.

Turquoise. Melon. Sand.

There were geometric shapes redolent of the Southwest in some of the prints and used as chic, subtle accents.

The clothes being modeled for her by beautiful, willowy creatures Emma would never look like were definitely in the style she'd developed for herself since moving to New Mexico, but high-end.

Sophisticated in a way she wouldn't have thought that particular style choice could be.

Emma gave Kon a considering look. "You do realize none of this is going to fit me the same as these models, right?"

For one thing, they were all size two with almost no busts, definitely no tummies and very little in the way of any behinds.

Emma's post-pregnancy body was a size twelve with a C-cup bust, a no longer flat tummy and hips that filled out her capris.

Kon let a heated gaze travel over Emma. "I'm counting on it. On you, they will look so much better."

One of the models got a little pickled look on her face, the one who had been trying to flirt with His Highness since her arrival. Another gave Emma an envious look, but one just smiled and sent Emma a discreet thumbs-up.

Emma couldn't help smiling back.

"Young love is so inspiring," one of the designer reps said, his expression filled with approval.

Lust more like, but Emma didn't correct the man.

"If you see something you like, we have everything in your size, available for you to try on or buy without trying, if that is your preference."

"Why would I buy clothes without trying them on?" Emma asked. "What if I don't like the way they look on me?"

"Anything you do not like will be returned or disposed of," Kon assured her.

"I don't even know how much these clothes cost." But nothing had price tags and that was a red flag toward *expensive* in Emma's book. "But *get rid of*? How spoiled are you?"

"In some ways, very," Kon admitted without hesitation or embarrassment. "I would feel even more spoiled if you were willing to try the clothes on for me in a private setting."

"You want me to give you a private fashion show?" she asked, blushing.

She couldn't help it. Here were professional models showing off the clothes for him and he was asking her to follow that?

"I would enjoy that very much, yes." The sensual timbre of his voice said he wasn't just planning to *watch*.

"Isn't that a little kinky?" she asked in a teasing tone, still embarrassed, but pleased too.

Because she could not doubt that the only woman in this room who interested Kon was Emma. Not some willowy model with perfect makeup and hair.

Someone coughed. Someone else made a strangled sound and one of the models just laughed right out loud. It was the one who had given Emma the thumbs-up.

And Emma realized she probably should not have said that about being kinky, even in a tease.

Kon just smiled though, his chocolate gaze filled with humor. "I'm pretty sure it takes more than wanting to see my lover try on her new clothes to make me kinky."

"You should be careful what you say," the oldest designer rep admonished Emma repressively. "Comments like that could give rise to all sorts of speculation in the media."

Kon turned a frown on the older woman. "But everyone in this room has signed nondisclosure agreements, have they not? Any leak will be dealt with punitively and quickly, I assure you," he said in freezing tones.

Then Kon leveled his gaze on each designer rep and model in turn. To a one, they all gave nods of assent.

Kon nodded his own head, like he was satisfied, and turned his attention back on Emma with a charming smile. "You have no need to censor yourself with me."

While the sentiment was lovely, Emma didn't agree. She didn't apologize for her words, instinctively knowing that would have invited Kon's wrath on the woman who had corrected Emma. However, she *did* think about what the older woman had said and determined to be more circumspect in her speech around others.

NDA signed, or not, things had a way of getting out. It was why Emma had been so careful in her wording of emails and messages when trying to get a hold of Kon to tell him about Mickey's imminent birth.

While she was sure both she and her Prince would always regret that he had not been part of Mickey's life from the beginning, she could not regret protecting Kon and his family from the media circus that knowledge of her pregnancy at that time would have created.

So far, they'd been left alone, but it suddenly struck Emma that once Mickey's existence was announced to the world in relation to him being Kon's son, that media circus would be inevitable.

"What?" Kon asked her, his expression concerned.

"I don't… What do you mean, *what*?"

"What were you just thinking that made your lovely face grow so pensive and not in a happy-contemplation way?" he asked, showing a perspicacity she wished he had not developed sometimes.

Emma looked around at everyone and then back at Kon. "Later."

He jerked his head in acknowledgment and then the fashion show recommenced.

Emma was judicious in her selections, but Kon was not. For every item she picked out, he added two to her growing closet.

Finally, Emma just said, "Stop. That's enough for

three women who *like* to dress up and change at least once a day."

"But you may not keep them all," he reminded her.

Like Emma had *any* intention of keeping even half of the clothes. "I can pretty much guarantee it." She rolled her eyes. "We could fund free lunches for at-risk children for two years with what you want to spend on clothes for me, I'm certain of it."

Even if she didn't know exactly how much each article cost, Emma knew the clothes they'd set aside already would cover more than her wages for the year. Or two.

"I'll make a deal with you."

"A deal?" Emma asked warily.

"Whatever I spend on your new wardrobe I will match as a donation to any charity of your choice."

Emma heard a couple of gasps, but her eyes were only for Kon. "You want me to spend more money?"

"We haven't gotten to the lingerie yet," he said with that look.

The one that turned her knees to water and sent sensations spiking through her core.

"And if I want to split the donations up?"

"Anything you like."

"Bring on the lingerie," Emma said with renewed enthusiasm.

Kon's laughter had her gaze sliding back to him.

"What?" she asked.

"You weren't particularly thrilled about the new designer clothes, but you are giddy with excitement at the thought of being able to donate to causes that you care about. You make me happy, Emma, *solnyshko*."

"I'm pretty happy right now too, Kon," she told him,

her mind whirling with ideas about whom she would donate the money to.

But moments later, she was blushing to beat the band, because Kon wanted to see Emma in every single piece of lingerie and made no bones about it.

Knowing that each item bought added to her fund for donations, Emma didn't want to say no, but it was getting ridiculous.

And embarrassing.

"I'm never going to wear something like that," she muttered as he instructed the designer rep to add a lacy corselette with garters for stockings to Emma's order.

"Why not?" Kon asked, sounding genuinely surprised.

"For one thing, I don't wear stockings or pantyhose."

"But on more formal occasions, you might find that you do."

"Attached to *that* corselette? I don't think so."

"Only you and I will know you're wearing something so sexy under your dress," he promised her.

"And that's supposed to make it better? I'll spend the whole time excited or embarrassed, or embarrassed because I'm excited."

Kon's expression said he saw no downside.

Emma shook her head. "No, Kon. I already said yes to those ridiculously tiny nightgowns that in no way are intended for sleeping comfortably."

"I'll give up one of the nighties if you get the corselette," he bargained.

"Seriously?" she asked, a little flummoxed that he was so keen for her to wear something like that.

She'd never worn any kind of sexy lingerie before.

"I'm very serious, I promise you." The expression

on his handsome face was enough to make Emma wish the entire entourage of designer reps and models to the moon.

Anywhere but here.

She swallowed. "Okay, I'll get the corselette." And she would wear it.

Because that look? That was worth stepping outside her comfort zone.

Konstantin walked into his room after his international conference call negotiating the rights for a new mineral source and nearly swallowed his tongue.

Emma lay on his bed reading a book, wearing one of his shirts. It was not a scene of over-the-top seduction, but the very domesticity of it got to him in ways nothing else would have. She was not even wearing one of the supersexy nightgowns he'd talked her into buying, but his instant erection said his body did not care.

Konstantin cleared his throat and Emma looked up from her book, her gaze unfocused and dreamy.

"Good book?" he asked.

"Yes." But she set it aside without hesitation, shifting to reveal that she wore a turquoise thong underneath his shirt.

Konstantin made no effort to stifle his groan of appreciation. "I thought you might go straight to bed."

He'd planned to join her in her room if she had, but didn't mention that. They'd had sex every night since their first physical reconnection and he had no desire to break that streak.

However, he'd been unable to get out of tonight's call.

Finding Emma waiting for him turned him on, no

question, but it touched something deep inside him as well.

"You would have just come looking for me." She smiled guilelessly up at him. "I thought this would be easier."

"You know me so well."

She slipped one button undone and smiled. "Oh, yes, I do."

"You look incredibly sexy in my shirt." If his voice had an underlying tone of surprise, he could be forgiven.

He'd talked her into the lingerie because he'd had plenty of fantasies about her wearing something like those pieces and yet, he could not imagine being more turned on than he was right at that moment.

Because Emma in *his* shirt felt right. And it was so damn sexy, his erection was pressing painfully against his slacks.

Her hands stilled in the efforts to unbutton the shirt. "Maybe I should leave it on." She gave him a flirty look.

And just like that, he was all in.

"Don't you dare." He stripped in record time, giving no care for his clothes falling in a wrinkled heap on the floor.

Emma undid the last button, her expression coy, her body sinuous against the bedding. Then she opened the shirt, revealing her gorgeous breasts, their peaks like ripe berries. His mouth watered to taste her.

The bright bit of silk that was her thong barely covered the apex of her thighs, but even that covering was too much.

Konstantin dived for her, his hands busy divesting her of the remaining clothing.

Her laughter cut off as he kissed her and what followed was intense and amazing and so incredibly satisfying.

But still, Emma went back to her own bed afterward like she always did.

Konstantin did not like it, but he did not know how to convince her that he would never let her down again like he had when he'd broken up with her.

And until he did, she wasn't risking Mickey's believing they were back together in a romantic capacity.

He respected her need to protect their son from potential heartbreak, but that didn't make it any easier for Konstantin to accept.

His brother had warned Konstantin he would have to work hard to rebuild his relationship with Emma.

The King had been frustratingly right.

Sitting on matching loungers, Emma and Kon took advantage of their last afternoon by the pool.

They watched their son swim and do tricks interspersed with the occasional, "Watch me, Mom. Look at this, Dad."

"He's amazing," Kon said, his voice heavy with love for their son.

"You know, when I was pregnant, I thought you'd be a great dad and then everything happened with not being able to reach you…"

"And having Tiana threaten you." His tone still carried guilt over that.

"Yes," Emma acknowledged, not sure how to alleviate Kon's guilt over a past that could not be changed. "I convinced myself then you wouldn't add anything good to Mickey's life."

"And now?"

She turned so their eyes met, his fixed on her with intense regard. Her answer mattered.

"Now, I think I was right when I thought you'd be a good dad. You really are, Kon." He was way more hands-on than she would have ever expected a workaholic like her Prince to be.

The fact he'd delegated responsibilities on both the company and palace front to free up time to get to know Mickey and help him acclimate to the changes in their lives said a great deal about Kon's dedication to fatherhood.

"I'm very glad you think so." Kon gave her one of his devastating smiles. "You know I believe you are the best mother our son could possibly have."

Emma wanted to believe that, but there was this tiny part of her that doubted. The part that could not forget she hadn't been enough before.

She was doing her best to let those feelings go, but they persisted and reared their ugly little heads at the worst times.

"He's really excited about the trip to Mirrus." Went unspoken was Emma's desperate hope Mickey's enthusiasm would not be dashed by the royal family's reaction to him, or to her.

"What about you? Are you looking forward to it?" Kon asked.

"Yes." She might have her trepidations, but she really was. Emma had craved access to Kon's life five years ago, now she was getting it. "I want to see where you grew up. I want to see the environment that helped define who you are, the place that will be so important to Mickey as he grows older. I want to know and understand Mirrus and its people."

And thereby maybe understand Kon a little better. She'd thought she'd known him before. She'd been wrong. Emma had been blind to both his acute sense of duty before all else and his ruthlessness when faced with making something happen.

Whether those traits were personal, cultural or fostered within his family, Emma wanted to know.

"You're such a special woman."

"Am I?"

"I think so, yes. You see the world from your own unique perspective and in that perspective my being a prince is only part of who I am, not the definition of who I am."

"Well, of course not. No single role can define any of us." Wouldn't life be boring if it did? "Even mine as Mickey's mom does not define me entirely."

Emma was also an artist, a bookkeeper, a friend… and a daughter, if estranged from her family. She was also Kon's lover. All those roles played some part in making her who she was and defining the parameters of her life.

"But it is the most important role to you at the present." He sounded very sure of that.

And, of course, he was right, only there was another role that was growing in importance to Emma. That of his lover and, possibly, one day his wife.

Not that she was saying so.

He had enough confidence without her giving any free boosts.

And because of Kon's generosity, Emma's art was consuming more of her time and talents in a good way, rejuvenating her and giving her an outlet for emotions she was in no way ready to acknowledge, much less express.

"Mickey is going to love having a grandfather, uncles and an aunt." Emma still felt guilty she'd done so little to build a family of adults for him to trust in and rely on.

Her son should never have had to pay for her introverted nature and fear of rejection.

Kon nodded, his expression showing full agreement. "And a cousin in a few months' time."

Emma smiled, remembering Mickey's reaction to that news. "He's over the moon about that one."

"He wants siblings." Kon said it like a warning.

As if Emma wouldn't know. "He told me." That had been an interesting conversation. Not least of which had been because of Mickey's final sally in that direction.

But what if Dad married someone else to give me a brother or sister? He wants more kids too, Mom.

Apparently Kon and Mickey had discussed it too. Which did not surprise her. Mickey could be very determined when his mind got set on something. What did surprise Emma was the shard of pain that sliced through her heart at the thought of Kon having children with someone else.

She'd thought she'd accepted that possibility long ago when he'd broken up with her so he could marry Nataliya. The marriage had never taken place, but Emma had prepared herself for the eventuality of it and what it would entail.

Or so she'd thought.

Her heart said, *Don't bet on it*, no matter what her

brain wanted to believe about Emma's emotional distance gained.

"Nataliya's mother is all set to play grandmother to him as well," Kon said, for once clearly oblivious to the direction Emma's thoughts had taken. "I think she and my father have something going on."

That piqued Emma's curiosity. "Really?" The former King, now Prince—Kon had explained that was the title his father had chosen upon abdication in favor of his eldest son—and the Countess?

"Well, Lady Solomia moved into our palace within a month of the marriage. And she seems very happy to be there."

"Her daughter is there… Isn't that reason enough?"

"The Countess and my dad spend a lot of time together." Kon sounded disgruntled and a little confused by that.

"Do you mind?"

"No." He grimaced. "Maybe a little, but I know I shouldn't. It's strange though." For once he did not look like a prince, but an adult man trying to come to terms with changes in his family he hadn't seen coming. "I don't know how either Nataliya or Nikolai feel about it."

Emma hid an indulgent smile. These moments when Kon showed his own imperfections made him feel more relatable and *touchable* in her life.

"I'm just glad Mickey is going to have some extended family, surrogate grandmother included." There would always be a part of Emma that wished her own parents could be in Mickey's life too. And her own.

She missed them.

"Would you want to renew your relationship with

your parents, if you could?" Kon asked, once again firmly on her wavelength.

"I think so. If I wasn't afraid of their rejection, I probably would have reached out to them again already," she admitted. "But that last phone call, it devastated me."

And she'd been absolutely unwilling to open Mickey's life to their potential rejection.

"They've had five years to miss you, to wonder about their grandchild."

"If they miss me at all." It was that *if* that made it impossible for Emma to contact them.

She'd missed them so badly after only the months of her pregnancy, she'd been sure their hearts would have softened. Emma had been wrong and hurt so very badly because of it.

"I'm sure they do." Kon sounded so convinced of his own belief.

Emma wished she could share it. "You never met them."

"But you talked about them. They love you."

"You couldn't tell that by the way they pushed me from their lives."

"Is that why you're hesitating about marrying me?" he asked. "Even though I'm asking for a future with you, you can't bring yourself to trust me. But it's not just what I did to you that you have to overcome," he said like he was discovering something new. "Your parents, the rest of your family…and me. We all did the same thing to you and all that emotion is still tangled."

He was right about the rest of her family. Emma had never been close to her cousins as they were so much older, but her aunts and uncles had always been wonderful to her. Until they all agreed to close ranks with her parents and shun her for keeping a baby without the benefit of marriage.

Kon was also right that all that pain and rejection were mixed up inside her.

Emma looked off into the distance, but the view of the mountains offered little solace and no answers. "You're pretty insightful for a prince."

"I'm also a COO, and believe me, both roles require insight into how the human psyche works."

"I suppose they do." She sighed. "I miss my parents. Still," she admitted. "They were good parents. I know they loved me, even if that love wasn't unconditional like mine is for Mickey." Emma could not imagine anything her son could do that would cause her to reject him.

"Maybe they saw themselves as loving you when they rejected you. Tough love."

She shrugged, wishing she could believe that. "All I know is that they rejected me and my son. And that still hurts."

Maybe her continued estrangement from her parents did play a significant role in Emma's refusal to commit to a lifetime with Kon.

Parents made a lifetime commitment when they had children, adopted or otherwise. Her parents had broken that commitment to Emma, and she didn't know if she could trust Kon to keep his promises in the future.

After all, they'd loved Emma and he did not.

Mickey's preschool graduation went off without a hitch. He absolutely glowed under all the compliments he got on his little suit and he told everyone it made him look like his dad.

When they arrived and everyone was getting settled before the ceremony began, Emma got teary eyed, watching her son take his place at the front of the banquet room.

She swiped at her eyes. "He's growing up so fast."

"Our little man," Kon agreed, his voice ringing with pride.

Emma smiled up at her Prince through the tears. "He's more excited about this than turning five."

Kon reflected her smile, reaching down to squeeze Emma's hand. "Naturally. That milestone is two months off. The immediate is always more exciting than something in the future."

A rush of emotion washed over Emma, making her tears spill over.

"Are you all right, *solnyshko*?" Kon asked with concern.

Swallowing, trying to get control of her wayward emotions, Emma nodded.

"Then why these tears?"

"That you know they are different than only a moment ago is kind of scary," she said on a hiccup.

"Good. Not scary."

She smiled. Her arrogant prince, so sure he knew what was best for her, but in this case, maybe he was right.

Maybe his knowing her so well *was* good.

"I've never had anyone to share his milestones with," she said in explanation. "I'm happy for Mickey." She gulped back more emotion. "And for me too."

"This is a very strange way to show happiness, *krasavitsa*."

"I'm hardly beautiful right now, with my mascara running." Her nose was probably pink too.

Kon handed her a handkerchief to mop herself up. "You are always beautiful to me, Emma."

"Why don't you say stuff like that to me?" a woman behind them asked her husband.

Emma recognized the voice as belonging to the mother of one of Mickey's friends he'd had playdates with. A woman with a wry sense of humor, Emma wasn't surprised she'd teased her husband that way.

"Because the last time I did you told me to get my eyes examined. Doesn't mean I'm not thinking it," her husband answered gamely.

Emma grinned at the exchange and shared a moment of rapport with Kon as humor shone in his eyes as well.

"I will always be there for the milestones, for both of you, from now on," Kon promised her, all serious again.

Emma choked up again, so all she could do was nod.

"These tears of yours are killing me," Kon told her.

She tried to blink them away. "I'm sorry."

Kon groaned and then kissed her. Right there in the middle of all the chatting parents waiting for the ceremony to start.

"That's my mom and dad," Mickey yelled.

Laughter erupted and Kon pulled back, his expression holding none of the humor from before. "I vow it."

Emma didn't know how to respond to that, so she ducked her head and then looked toward their son, who was giving her a thumbs-up. If she didn't watch out,

Mickey would be planning their wedding before they ever got to Mirrus.

And would that be such a terrible thing? a small voice in her head asked.

Mickey was an absolute gem on the trip to his father's homeland. Of course, the fact that Kon had made sure he had plenty to entertain him *and* a nap en route helped loads.

Emma was instructed to simply relax and she tried, even taking her own nap, but the closer they got to their destination, the more anxious she grew.

Kon took her hand and brought it to his mouth to kiss it. He'd been a lot more publicly affectionate since the kiss in front of Mickey's school the previous evening.

Their son knew they were *dating* and Kon saw no reason to pretend they were not as close as they were. Or so he said when she'd questioned him about the good-morning kiss he'd given her at breakfast.

Emma had still insisted on sleeping in her own bed the night before though.

Actually sleeping with Kon, allowing their son to find them in the same bed in the morning, would signify a level of commitment from her she was still hesitant to make.

"Is it going to be a media circus at the airport?" she asked him, drumming a tattoo with her fingers against the armrest.

Kon reached out and stilled her fingers with his hand over hers. "Relax, *solnyshko*. No media circus. My family will be waiting at the palace for us. Not because they do not want to meet our plane but because we can land unremarked this way."

She nodded, like that made sense, only really? Emma had never been exposed to the public side of Kon's life. And her own life had never had that component.

So, honestly, she had no idea.

"We will make the announcement about Mickey at the end of our first week on Mirrus. I want you to get to know my family in relative privacy before the media catch wind of our son's existence and start asking intrusive questions."

"It would be easier on all of you if you could announce our marriage at the same time, wouldn't it?" she asked, trying not to feel guilty.

She had to do what was best for her *and* Mickey, she told herself.

"I am not interested in what is easy for me," Kon assured her. "I am only concerned with what makes you comfortable. When you agree to marry me, it will be because that is what *you* want, not because it is an expedient public relations move."

"You know I really appreciate you haven't tried to guilt me into agreement." She acknowledged to herself it would probably work at this point.

It wouldn't have before. Not when they'd first reconnected, but her heart had softened and so much of the resentment she'd carried toward Kon was gone now.

"I would not."

"Thank you. I believe you."

"I've spoken to my father, but even so I cannot promise he will not attempt it," Kon admitted with a rueful twist of his lips and no small amount of frustration. The man liked to be in control. "He's very good at guilt trips."

"He must be." Prince Evengi had used them to coerce Kon into not only signing that blighted marriage contract but also breaking up with Emma to follow through on it.

"Remember, he is as susceptible to them as his sons. If he gets too pushy, just remind my father that if it were not for his insistence I follow through on that contract, you and I would have been married long ago."

"You say that now."

"I say it because it is true," Kon said forcefully, like it really bothered him she still doubted on that score. "Seeing how I am with our son, can you doubt I would have moved heaven and earth to be his father from the moment I learned of his existence?"

Emma was saved answering that emotionally charged question by the captain coming over the loudspeaker of the private royal jet to instruct them on preparing for landing.

CHAPTER TEN

WHILE THERE WERE no other royals or dignitaries in evidence when Kon, Emma and Mickey disembarked from the plane, there was an entire second security detail and three imposing SUVs with a limousine slotted in between the first and third ones.

"Wow! Do we get to ride in the limo?" Mickey asked excitedly.

"Yes. It has been fitted with a child safety seat for Mikhail," Kon told Emma before she could even ask.

"I have no doubt." Emma was wearing one of the designer outfits Kon had bought her and Mickey was all decked out in one of his tailored suits.

He'd changed after his nap on the plane.

Emma was tense on the ride to the palace, though her attention was fixed keenly on the view out the window, as she got her first view of Kon's homeland.

There were similarities to where she'd grown up outside Seattle. The same towering evergreens and lush deciduous summer vegetation. The mountains in the distance were snow-capped and she knew that there were glaciers on the island.

Kon had been right to warn her that the temperatures were not what they were in New Mexico. Although it was summer, there was a chilly wind that the evening sun could not make up for. Emma shivered, wishing she'd put a jacket on.

Then warm fabric fell around her shoulders and she looked up to find Kon smiling at her. "Better?"

He stood there in his shirtsleeves, which she was sure went against protocol, but didn't even shiver.

She nodded. "Thank you."

Emma tried to give him back his suit jacket when they got settled inside the limo, but Kon shook his head. "Keep it on. You still look chilled."

"Did my blue lips give me away?" she teased. It wasn't *that* cold, but it was by no means warm either.

At least outside. The limo was comfortable, but Emma found herself too willing to keep Kon's jacket, like a security blanket, around her. His delicious scent reminded her that she was here at his invitation and *for* him and their son.

She might not be a princess, but she belonged here because she *was* Mickey's mom and maybe even because she was the woman Kon wanted to marry.

Even if it was for the sake of their son.

"It's not that cold, Mom. My suit keeps me warm anyway," Mickey informed her. "Like Dad."

"A good-quality suit has many uses," Kon said, like imparting great wisdom.

Emma bit back a smile as their son nodded sagely. These two.

"They're going to like me, right, Dad? I'm going to have a grandpa now, right, Mom?"

Emma was surprised it had taken this long for Mickey's nerves to show up. And a little impressed. His mother had been a nervous wreck for hours. Nevertheless, she gave him her most reassuring smile. "Yes, a grandfather, two uncles and an aunt."

"They are going to love you just as I do," Kon assured their worried son.

"They have to, don't they? I'm their family."

Emma did not mention that family did not always love as they should. She just nodded.

Their first view of the palace left Emma speechless. She'd seen it in pictures, but up close? It was awe-inspiring.

"Wow, it's so big!" Mickey was not similarly afflicted. "Did you get lost lots when you were a little boy?" he asked his father.

Kon shook his head. "No. Nikolai took me exploring from my earliest memory, making sure I knew where I could go and shouldn't go and how to get back to the nursery. He and I did the same for our younger brother, Dima."

"Don't only babies live in nurseries?" Mickey asked.

"Not in the palace. The nursery is the room with toys and room for a train set on the floor. I lived in it until I was a teenager and then I got my own suite. I was given an apartment in the palace when I graduated from university."

"Will I have my own apartment in the palace some day?"

"I do not know. It depends on how much of the year you live in Mirrus. Palace apartments are reserved for adult family that live here year-round."

"But you don't. Do you still have an apartment?"

"I do." Kon didn't offer to explain why.

Emma was glad. Mickey might not act like it, but he was already on information overload. The way his gaze flitted everywhere and landed nowhere indicated nerves her son wasn't giving voice to.

"Will I stay in the nursery?" Mickey asked, sounding like he wasn't sure he liked that idea.

"I had a room in my apartment prepared for you to stay in, but if you would rather stay in the nursery, you can."

"I want to stay with you." Mickey frowned. "What about Mom?"

"Your mother has a suite across the hall from us." It was Kon's turn to sound slightly disgruntled by *that* reality. "You can stay with her if you would rather. A bed can be put in her sitting room for you."

"Why isn't she staying with us? We're a family!" Mickey's volume was startling and unexpected.

Emma and Kon reached out at the same time to touch him in comfort. She took Mickey's little hand in her own and Kon laid his big hand on Mickey's shoulder.

"I had my own room at the house in Santa Fe, Mickey."

"But that was different. That house was *ours*. The King owns the palace, only the apartment is Dad's. You should be in it with us. I'll sleep on the couch. You can have my room."

"And this is important to you, that we are all in a space that is *ours*?" Kon asked, like he was trying to understand what prompted Mickey's outburst.

"Yes!" Mickey was adamant.

Kon looked to Emma. If she was reading him correctly, he would follow her lead.

She looked around the limo just a little wildly, worried that the door was going to open any moment and there would be no more privacy for this conversation.

"I will not give the signal to open the door until we are settled on this matter," Kon said, proving that once again, they were very much in tune.

Emma let out a little sigh of relief. "Let's get you unbuckled," she said to Mickey.

Like she expected him to, her son insisted on undoing the five-point harness on his own. The act of doing something so familiar should help him calm down a little while Emma's brain scrambled for a solution to his clear upset.

"Why don't you sit here, between your dad and me, so we can all figure out our feelings right now." Undoing her own seat belt, Emma scooted over to make room for him between her and Kon.

Mickey moved into the opening rapidly, showing he was in need of both physical and emotional reassurance. "Mom, I don't want you to stay in a suite. Someone might think you aren't part of our family."

Emma did not tell him that was a silly thought. She'd discovered that children's minds had their own brand of logic. He drew his conclusions based on how he understood the world. She would try to help him with that understanding, but she would not dismiss his worries, even if they did not make sense to her.

"Mikhail Ansel Carmichael, I need you to hear me. No one is going to question that I am your mom, your family."

Mickey chewed on his lip. "Why does Dad have a different name from me and you?"

Emma opened her mouth and then closed it, wishing she always had just the right answer for her son. Only she didn't. "Your dad and I aren't married, but even if we were, I might choose to keep my own last name."

"Really?"

"Really."

"Why?"

Emma shrugged. "Because it's mine. Because I want to. It's my choice."

"Do I get to choose my last name?" Mickey asked.

Emma cast a quick glance at Kon, who looked pained. "You are in the royal succession. Your name will have to legally be changed to Merikov," Kon answered.

"Oh. That's okay."

"It is?"

"Yes, then everyone will know you are my dad."

"You are not worried they will not know Emma is your mom?" Kon asked, like the words were drawn from him.

"No. She's always been my mom. She tells everybody." Mickey frowned. "But some people won't know she's yours too. She has to stay with us, Dad, in *our* place."

Emma knew it! Mickey already had her married, even if the wedding hadn't take place yet, much less her agreement to it.

"I do not belong to your dad," Emma told her son, but the words felt like a lie.

Instead of getting upset that she'd disagreed, Mickey rolled his eyes. "You're my mom."

"Yes."

"He's my dad."

"Yes."

"You belong to each other because of me."

"Mickey, you know some parents are not together."
He'd known the Jensens, seen the parents separate and

divorce. More than that, he'd had friends in his preschool that came from unconventional families where the mom and dad had never even been a couple.

Mickey shrugged. "You and Dad are together. You kissed. Everybody saw you."

She knew that would come back to bite her. Only she couldn't regret that Kon had shown her affection in that moment. It had felt so spontaneous, so right.

"Yes, we kissed, but we aren't engaged, or anything."

"Mom, I think you need to figure out your feels."

Oh, man. He was so right. Emma needed to figure out her feelings for sure, but right now she still had to deal with Mickey's need for her to stay in Kon's apartment with him and his father.

Kon's stifled snicker said he agreed with their son.

She gave her Prince a pointed glare. "I agree, Mickey. I do need to figure out my emotions and having my own space will help me do that."

"You can have my bedroom in Dad's apartment."

"Why give up your bedroom when I have a perfectly good suite across the hall?"

"Because we're a family," Mickey replied stubbornly.

"I hear you, Mickey, and I care very much that you feel secure in our new environment—"

"She talks like this when she's going to say *no*," Mickey told his father, interrupting her. "Don't say *no*, Mom. I don't wanna be scared."

"Scared, why scared?" Kon asked.

"I don't know." Mickey's eyes filled with tears. "I just know I want you and Mom both safe in *our* place."

"The whole palace is safe, I promise you," Kon said, his tone filled with reassuring calm.

"Please, Mom. Please," Mickey said, clearly unable to express why he needed this so badly.

Emma hugged her son tight. "Listen, Mickey, I don't understand why this is so important to you. I don't think you understand it either, but what I do know is that you've had a lot of changes in a short amount of time. And maybe that has you feeling insecure. I'll sleep on Kon's couch if that will make you feel better."

She wasn't a prima donna who needed her own suite of rooms.

"I will have an extra bed brought into my room, there is plenty of space," Kon said, all autocratic prince.

Before Emma could even reply, Mickey was jerking from Emma's arms to hug his dad. "That would be so great, Dad. Thank you! I know Mom will be safe if she's in your room."

Emma wanted to laugh at the gallows humor of that one because one thing she knew, her heart would *not* be safe with her staying in Kon's bedroom.

The interior of the palace was everything Emma could have expected it to be. Marble floors in the grand foyer, twin curved staircases up to the next floor and gold accents everywhere.

Her artist's eye told her that that gold was genuine leaf and not just paint.

But it was the people waiting to meet her and Mickey that drew her attention. She recognized Prince Evengi, King Nikolai and the Princess of Mirrus, Nataliya, from pictures, as well as Prince Dimitri, whom the family called Dima and looked more like Nikolai than Konstantin.

Nataliya's mother, the Countess, was the only other

person present who was not security. No dignitaries. No staff. This was a meeting between family and only family.

Emma found a great deal of comfort in the fact even a royal family understood the need for this kind of intimate gathering.

"It is such a pleasure to finally meet you." Nataliya took Emma's hands in both of hers and pressed a kiss to each of Emma's cheeks. "Konstantin is so different since finding you again."

"He seems very much the same to me," Emma admitted.

Which was both worrying and comforting at the same time.

The King took his wife's place in front of Emma. "I need you to know that my deceased wife did not have my support in her plans for your child. She would never have gotten my approval to threaten you the way she did."

"Thank you for saying that." Emma had no idea how much she'd needed to hear those words from the King's own lips. "Mickey is my life."

"And now you are both my brother's."

Emma did not reply to that, but looked where her son was interacting with his grandfather for the first time. Prince Evengi had seemed very stiff and formal when introductions had been made, but he knelt on the floor with his grandson now, intent on whatever Mickey was saying.

Emotion swelled inside Emma.

Kon had made this possible. He had given Mickey a family and he'd done it without ever once threatening Emma's place in Mickey's life.

She wasn't stupid. She knew that he could have gone for custody of their son. He might not have won. It would have been an ugly battle, but never once had Kon ever even implied he wanted Mickey without Emma.

And there could be no question that Kon wanted his child in his life. He was such a devoted father.

Kon's own unwillingness to bend, the threats of Queen Crazy and Emma's own fears had cost them five years apart.

In that moment of clarity, Emma realized it wasn't enough to say she didn't want to act out of fear any longer. She had to actually do things differently to honor that desire.

There would be no more time apart. No more waffling on building a family together, not just building individual relationships between Mickey and his father.

"Konstantin was moved beyond words that you named Mikhail for him."

"It felt right at the time," Emma said, repeating something she'd told Kon once.

"Thank you for being such a good mother to my nephew and for giving my brother a chance to be in his life."

Emma finally turned her gaze back to the King. "You do not have to thank me for being a decent person."

"I think I do. I was married to the woman who threatened you. I know we are not all motivated by what is best for our family and those we are supposed to care about."

Emma's eyes widened. If she was not mistaken, the King was telling her that his marriage to Queen Crazy had not been all sunshine and roses. "Do you know why she wanted my baby so badly?"

"She never wanted to be pregnant. I think she saw your baby as her easy way out of something she did not want."

Emma nodded. That made sense. "Kon always thought she was too young to take on the role of queen."

"He talked to you about her?"

"Yes. Before, when we were living together."

"Before he dumped you," Nataliya said from near Emma's shoulder. "To marry me." The Princess of Mirrus rolled her eyes. "Like that was ever going to work."

A laugh was startled out of Emma. "Some people obviously thought it would."

"Some people were wrong." Nataliya didn't sound the least apologetic about making that pronouncement. "I owe Konstantin an apology though."

"Why?" Emma and the King asked at the same time.

Nataliya looked up at her husband, the love she held for him so clear to see and that it was reciprocated could not be doubted. The King looked besotted. "I judged your brother as a playboy when all the time he was nursing a broken heart from giving up his *One True Thing.*"

"I'm not that," Emma denied immediately. "Kon doesn't love me."

"If you say so." But Nataliya sounded like she did not agree.

"He told me so." But did it matter?

That was the question Emma really had to answer. Did it matter if Kon loved her, or if he did love her, if he was ever able to recognize that?

She loved him. She always had. Always would. And

that was why she had not dated. It had not just been fear of rejection. Or being too busy raising and providing for their son.

But because Emma *had* found her *One True Thing* and had always known that anything less in a relationship would not be enough.

"Nik told me that he didn't love me either. Before we married." Nataliya gave the King a look of indulgence that made him grimace.

"You, of course, were fully aware of your own feelings."

Color washed into Nataliya's cheeks. "That is not the point."

Emma smiled at the royal couple, so much less intimidated than she'd expected to be by them. "No, the point is that when you love someone, you take risks with your heart even when you're scared."

Nataliya's eyes widened. "Um, yes? Sure, that was the point I was trying to make."

Emma smiled at the other woman, suddenly sure that she and this person who had always stood in her own mind between Emma and her happiness would be a great friend.

"If it helps you at all, I am certain my brother will never let you down again," Nikolai said, like a sibling who cared and with just a smidgen of the arrogance of a king.

Emma nodded. "You know? I think you may be right."

That night Emma and Kon tucked Mickey into bed together as they'd done every night since that fateful morning in the bank.

"You're staying on the couch, right, Mom?" Mickey asked drowsily.

"I'm staying here, in the apartment with you and your dad. We'll all have breakfast together when you wake up."

"Mmm, 'kay…" Mickey snuggled down into his blankets and fell asleep just like that.

"He is exhausted."

"It was an eventful and emotional-filled day. He got an adoring grandfather, surrogate grandmother, two uncles and an aunt all in one fell swoop." Emma turned off the bedside lamp, noting that Kon had already turned on Mickey's night-light.

They stood at the same time and headed out of the dim room.

"My father is like a child himself in his excitement over getting to know Mikhail." Kon sounded both pleased by that and indulgent toward his father.

"He calls him Mishka too." They all did.

Kon made an *mmm* sound. "It is a sign of affection to use the diminutive."

"I think that's why I've pushed back against calling him Mikhail. Every time I say Mickey, it's like I'm saying I love him."

"He may not realize that in his head, but his little-boy heart hears the words, *solnyshko*."

Emma walked into Kon's bedroom and then turned to face him. "Am I still your sunshine?"

"Can you doubt it?" Kon asked, his dark gaze serious and intense. "You have brought the light back into my life."

"Mickey shines pretty brightly too."

Kon pulled Emma to him, their bodies touching,

and kissed her gently before smiling. "I adore our son, *krasavitsa*, but it is *you* who brings light into all the dark places in my soul."

For once, Emma did no mental gymnastics to dismiss how loving his words sounded. She simply soaked them in and accepted them as they were.

"You sound so Russian right now," she told him with a small smile.

"Mirrussian."

"Mirrussian," she corrected herself and reached up to kiss him. "My Mirussian prince."

"Solnyshko moi."

No more words followed. Only kissing and touching. Emma felt cherished as Kon divested her of her clothing. She returned the favor, caressing his gorgeous body with a sense of possessiveness she'd not allowed herself before now.

He *was* hers. And she *was* his. And that truth had not changed in their five years apart.

"I forgive you," she said against his skin as she mapped his sculpted torso with her lips.

Konstantin stilled, instant comprehension thrumming through his body. She *forgave* him.

Suddenly their slow loving was not enough. He needed all of Emma. Now.

He flipped them and leaned down to kiss her passionately. "Thank you." He kissed her all over her beautiful face, thanking her over and over again between each press of his lips against her silky skin.

Emma grabbed his cheeks and held his head so their eyes met. "I mean it, Kon. I forgive you for breaking up with me. I forgive you for the other women. You're right that we belonged to each other, but I was right too. We *weren't* together and you did not owe me fidelity. You do now though," she said with a look that would have intimidated better men than him.

"You are it for me. For the rest of our lives."

Her smile was blinding. "For the rest of our lives." She rubbed her thumbs over his face and he moaned. She was still naked under him, after all. "Breaking up with me is what hurt me. Not letting me contact you afterward. That cost all of us, but believe me when I say that I forgive you for all of it. No more crushing guilt. No more letting the past get in the way of our future."

Was she saying what it sounded like? "You're going to marry me?"

"Is that a proposal?"

"You know it is." Konstantin felt like kicking himself. "I know it's not a romantic moment in Central Park, damn it." Konstantin was *not* his damn brother. His patience had a hell of a lot more limits. "I should do better. But I need to know now."

Another blinding and beautiful smile sent his already stiff erection to rock-hard status. "Yes, Kon, I will marry you. You and Mickey aren't the only ones who want to give him a younger sibling."

What happened after that would not live in his moments of pride for his vaunted control, because Konstantin had none. No control left, he made love to his sunshine like a starving man feasting on her every gasp and moan of pleasure.

He drove them both to the height of pleasure and then over, only to do it all again.

His hunger refused to be sated with a single bout of lovemaking. Or even two. He and Emma finally fell into an exhausted sleep after their third time joining their bodies and their souls in a union he had never known with another woman.

Mickey's squeal brought Emma out of sleep better than any alarm clock.

She sat straight up and realized with instant relief that someone had put a nightgown on her. It wasn't her usual boring T-shirt-style garment, but it covered the important bits and made this morning greeting with her son relaxed rather than awkward.

Gratitude for Kon's thoughtfulness filled her even as she grinned at her son. "Got something to say, Mickey?"

"You're in Dad's bed! I knew it would work," Mickey crowed.

"What would work?" Kon asked from the other side of the bed.

"If Mom stayed here with us, she'd see."

"See what?" Emma asked her precocious son.

"That me and Dad, we're both your family. You're supposed to be together."

"You think so, huh?" Emma teased, not at all bothered that her son had been matchmaking again.

His distress the day before had been genuine and maybe it had been sparked by fear of her separating herself from Kon, or just plain old insecurity. Emma didn't care. She loved her son. She loved his father. She wanted a life together as a *real family*, as Mickey called it, more than just about anything.

"He looks like he wants to kiss you all the time," Mickey said with a roll of his eyes.

"You're very insightful, Mishka. How does your mom look at me?" Kon asked in a humor-laden tone.

"Like she wants to trust you. Like after I do something bad and I'm really sorry, but she has to make me go to my room and think about it anyway."

Their son *was* insightful. Emma put her arms out and Mickey joined them on the bed without hesitation, snuggling between her and Kon. "From now on, I'm going to look at your dad like I want to kiss him all the time too. What do you think about that?"

"That's kinda gross, but you're grown-ups so it's okay, I guess."

Kon and Emma shared laughter.

"It is more than okay," Kon assured him. "It is everything good."

The rest of that week was filled with family bonding and Emma learning what her life as part of the royal family would be like.

She would have to take classes in etiquette and get coaching on public relations, politics and a bunch of other stuff that frankly didn't sound very fun.

She would do it though, just like she'd gotten her degree in bookkeeping.

Emma hadn't particularly enjoyed those courses either, but she'd learned what she needed to be the best mom she could be for Mickey. So she could provide for him.

This was much the same. Only she had both Mickey and Konstantin's welfare to think about.

Nataliya, who had insisted that Emma drop the honorific unless they were in a formal setting, took a personal role in helping Emma slide into her role as future Princess.

As Kon had told her, it was up to the King whether to confer that title to Emma upon her marriage to his brother and King Nikolai had made it clear he intended to do so.

Mickey had been in alt.

Emma not so much. But, princess or duchess, she had to learn the role and she was committed to doing so.

The royal family planned to introduce her and Mickey to the rest of the world at a banquet for the country's most elite dignitaries, nobility and business associates. The wedding would take place in only a month's time.

Emma hadn't balked at the rapidity of it all, hoping that less time to prepare would equate to a smaller event.

Nataliya, who was fast becoming a very dear friend, had told Emma not to bet on it. Her mom had gotten all the practice she'd needed on Nataliya's speedy wedding and had stepped in to plan this one with an almost frightening glee.

Emma ached a little, wishing her own mom were there to put her own two cents in, but tried to quash thoughts like that.

Her life was so blessed, Emma didn't want to dim the joy she could have by grieving what she could not change.

CHAPTER ELEVEN

"ARE YOU SURE you shouldn't have warned Emma about this?" Nikolai asked after Kon told his brother he needed him to cover a meeting so he could go to the airport and greet the arrival of Emma's estranged parents.

"I didn't tell her I planned to contact them in case they were no more interested in renewing their relationship with their daughter than they were five years ago."

Nikolai snorted. "She's marrying a prince. I'm pretty sure that changes things for them."

"I didn't tell them about the upcoming wedding. It would hurt Emma to find out they only agreed to see her and Mickey because she was going to be *respectable* again." Konstantin hadn't told the elderly couple that he was a prince either.

Just a friend of Emma's who hoped to see the estrangement ended.

"And they still agreed to come?"

"They jumped at it. They miss their daughter so much. Her mother cried and begged me to promise I wasn't tricking them."

"If they missed her so much, why let the separation go on so long?"

"They couldn't find her." Apparently her parents had run into the same difficulty Konstantin had when they'd finally decided to look for their daughter.

They didn't know the name of their grandson. Didn't know she'd changed her last name. Didn't know she'd moved out of state.

"How did you explain them needing to come to Mirrus to see her?" Nikolai asked.

"I told her that this is where she and Mikhail were living right now."

"Technically, that is true."

"If not the entire truth, yes. Mirrus will always be home for my family."

"You just love saying that, don't you?"

"What?" Konstantin asked, but he knew.

"*Your family.* I am truly sorry that five years ago you did not feel you could come to me and tell me that this woman was your family."

"I didn't recognize it then. I wouldn't let myself. That is not on you, or our father. That is on me, but she's forgiven me and the past is no longer a weight around my neck, choking me."

"I know you. You still feel guilty."

"I am trying not to."

"Because she wants you to."

Konstantin didn't bother responding. His brother knew him well enough to know that was exactly it. For Emma's sake, Konstantin was doing his best to let go of the guilt that his own ruthlessness had caused.

And maybe one day, when she loved him again and wasn't just prepared to become a family for their son's sake, he would.

* * *

Emma was enjoying a rare moment alone in their apartment in the palace.

Mickey was visiting with his grandfather and Lady Solomia. Kon was at work and for this moment, Emma had no classes on etiquette or meetings with wedding purveyors. How they were managing to keep a lid on her and Mickey's existence while going forward with wedding plans was mind-boggling to Emma.

The loyalty of the palace staff had to be amazingly deep.

Or their NDAs were truly punitive in a way no one wanted to risk invoking.

Either way, Emma needed a moment to catch her breath.

So, when a knock sounded on her door, she grimaced, not really wanting to talk to anybody. Not even Nataliya.

Sighing, Emma got up to go to the door, only to have it open before she reached it.

Konstantin stood on the other side, two people behind him.

"Why did you knock?" she asked before registering the identity of the people with him.

Her parents? Her parents were *here*. In Mirrus.

"Mom?" she asked, her voice barely above a whisper. "Dad?"

And then her mother rushed around Kon and ran to Emma, pulling her into a hug so tight Emma could barely breathe. "My baby. My daughter. I'm sorry. I'm so sorry." The litany of apologies did not end when her dad joined them, only intensified as he added his voice to her mother's.

Emma pushed out of her parents' arms and took a step back. "You're here."

Her mother's eyes shone brightly with tears. "Yes. Your friend called us and told us this is where you are living now."

"I started looking for flights right away," her dad said, clearing his throat. "But he said he could get us on a private jet sooner than a commercial flight could get us here."

Emma looked at Kon and mouthed the word *friend*?

Kon nodded, but what did that mean?

"Why are you here?" she asked her parents, still trying to understand what was happening.

"You're here. We missed you so much," her mother said.

Her father got that look he did when he was feeling emotional and didn't want to show it. "We made a mistake when we pushed you away. We should never have done that. You're our daughter and you should *always* have been able to rely on our support."

"Did Kon tell you that?"

"You mean Mr. Merikov?" her mother asked, making no effort to hide the tears tracking down her face. "No, though I'm sure he's thought it if he's your friend. We missed you and we couldn't find you."

"You looked?" Emma asked, shocked.

"Oh, yes, but we couldn't find you. We thought maybe you'd gotten married and changed your name, but there was no marriage record in Washington or the surrounding states. We even had our private investigator check into Nevada marriages. So many people get married in Las Vegas."

Disappointment filled Emma. "So, that's why you're

here. You found out I'm getting married and now I'm acceptable to you."

Her mom gasped, her hand fisting over her heart. "You're getting married? To who?"

"You do not need to be married to be acceptable to us," her father said forcefully at the same time. "You are our daughter and we will always love you."

"Then why reject me?" Emma asked, the pain inside her lacing her voice.

"We thought if we stayed strong you would see we were right. You were so young, not even done with college yet. You had your whole life ahead of you and we thought being a single mom would make it so much harder than it had to be," her mom tried to explain.

"I was a fool," her father said, sounding tired and sad. "I thought you refusing to give your baby up for adoption was your way of saying that being adopted wasn't the best thing for you. I felt like you were rejecting me as your father. I was so darn selfish and I have no excuse."

Emma stared at her father, incomprehension holding her immobile. He'd believed she didn't like that she was adopted and that's why she wanted to keep her baby?

"I kept Mikhail because I already loved him, because I could not imagine giving him up and I knew that even if it was hard, I would and could give him a good life. I could give him what you'd always given me. Love."

Her mother started crying in earnest then. Emma found herself back in her mother's arms, her own tears coming to the surface. Her dad held them both.

But as the storm of healing weeping ended, Emma

sought out the one person she needed more than her parents right then. Kon.

He was there, waiting patiently.

After extricating herself from her parents' arms again, this time with words of love and promises they would work things out, she went to her fiancé and let him draw her into his embrace.

"Thank you," she said against his chest, finding immeasurable comfort in Kon's hold.

"Oh, you are going to marry Mr. Merikov?" her mother asked in a water-clogged voice.

Emma looked up, giving her mother a smile that was not strained at all. "Yes. Mom, Dad... I want you to meet my fiancé, His Royal Highness Prince Konstantin of the House of Merikov."

She peeked up at Kon. "Did I get that right?"

"Perfect," he said with a warm smile. "Now you tell me their names."

"Even though you already know them?"

He shrugged. "Etiquette."

Emma nodded. Okay, then. "Kon, may I present my parents? Ansel and Belinda Sloan."

Her mother was staring at Emma like a landed fish, her mouth opening and closing with nothing coming out.

Her dad's eyes widened. "Well, I'll be damned. And he doesn't mind about Mikhail?" he then said pointedly to Kon. "You will accept my grandson as your own?"

"Even if he were not mine, yes, I would."

"You're the man that..." Oh, her dad's eyes could still glitter with pure disapproval and it was all directed at Kon. "You seduced our innocent daughter and then abandoned her?"

"I did," Kon said unequivocally. "That is my mistake to bear, but believe me when I promise you that I will never let her down that way again."

"I should hope not," her mother said, sounding discombobulated. "A prince." She shook her head. "And you managed to keep his identity private?"

The discussion that followed was filled with explanations and updates. Her parents were hurt to learn Emma had changed her name to her birth surname, but had understood the need after learning about the restraining order.

"You just make me so proud," her mom said. "You're such a good mom."

Emma thought her heart would burst at those longed-for words coming from her parent.

"You make us both proud. We don't deserve your forgiveness, but I hope we can earn it over time."

"Your daughter excels at extending grace," Kon said before Emma could assure her parents she would forgive them.

There was a moment Emma found humorous, even if the others did not. Kon demanded promises never to hurt her again from her parents while her father assured Kon that *he* would be watching the younger man to make sure he never let their beloved daughter down again.

Emma rolled her eyes. "All this posturing is lovely, I'm sure, but please, all of you, remember that I did an excellent job looking out for myself and my son for five years."

Her mother's expression turned hungry. "I understand you're hesitant to allow it right away. We'll have to prove ourselves… But when do you think we might meet our grandson?"

"You want to meet Mickey?"

"Oh, yes. He's part of you. He's part of *us*. It's my own fault, but I've grieved knowing I had a grandchild out there I did not know for the past five years."

Emma didn't remind her mom about the phone call after Mickey's birth. The older woman was already filled with repentance. She did not need another load of guilt.

"You don't have to prove yourselves. You've said you're sorry and I believe you. I can still remember all the years of my childhood and how loved I felt. I know who you two are and it's not people who want to hurt others."

She might never fully understand what drove them to be the way they were five years ago, but she had some inkling after the watershed talking they'd done.

Her parents meeting with Mickey was emotional in all the best ways. They had relaxed some of their strict attitudes in the five years since Emma disappeared from their lives.

They wanted nothing more than to get to know their grandson and reacquaint themselves with their daughter.

No question, they were a little overwhelmed by the whole royal thing.

However, Emma's mom readily participated in the wedding preparations with Lady Solomia. Emma overheard the countess tell her mom that parents sometimes made grievous mistakes with their children, but the lucky ones had daughters who understood that they were loved and gave that love back, despite their parents' failings.

Emma thought there was a story there, but she didn't

go digging for it. She had enough to keep her occupied keeping up with her own life.

Mickey thrived as his family expanded in the days leading up to the royal wedding.

Kon and his family did an excellent job of shielding not only Mickey but also Emma from the media interest the announcement of their existence sparked.

Her wedding was over the top with way more guests than she'd anticipated, but Emma didn't mind.

Because the only two people who really registered with her were Kon and Mickey. Looking so proud he could bust his buttons, Mickey stood as Kon's best *man*. They both waited, their attention fixed entirely on her, as Emma walked forward to join them and the priest.

She spoke her vows with conviction and a lot of emotion she wasn't surprised to feel. Emma loved this man to the very depth of her soul and adored her son. Kon spoke his vows with an intense emotion that Emma had a very difficult time *not* calling love.

This moment wasn't just about Kon and Emma and their commitment to each other, but it was about Mickey too. Their commitment to him and any future children they might have together.

And the little boy knew it. He'd insisted on making his own promises as part of the ceremony, to the obvious delight of the attendees.

Kon and Emma surprised Mickey with vows of their own to him and including each other.

It was a really special moment and the number of guests, the camera crews… None of it mattered as Emma gave and received vows that would govern the rest of her life and that of her little family.

* * *

Konstantin did not know what was wrong with him, but throughout his wedding and the reception that followed, he kept getting overwhelmed by emotion.

He would go to speak to someone and have to pause, take a breath and get his feelings under control. It was unlike anything he'd ever experienced, but his relief… his utter joy that Emma had not only agreed to be his wife, but had genuinely forgiven him knew no bounds.

She had promised everything that mattered during their wedding vows, looking him right in the eye when she said she would *love* and honor and cherish him for the rest of their lives.

He needed to get her alone, to ask if that meant what he thought. Even more important, he needed to tell her that he loved her.

It had struck him as she approached him and Mishka at the church. She'd looked so beautiful, but it was the light shining from inside her that completely took his breath away.

In that moment, he'd accepted that he *needed* her, that she sat as firmly in his soul as any member of his family, including their son, but that she was the one person he craved above all others as part of his life.

He loved Mishka and would be the best dad he could be, but it was Emma who gave their little family heart.

Coming up behind her, Konstantin slid his arm around her waist in a very uncool show of affection.

Emma gasped, like his action surprised her. And it should. This did not fall under proper protocols for public behavior.

And for once, he did not care.

He needed to be close to her.

"Hello, *solnyshko moi*. Are you enjoying yourself?"

Emma had been talking to Nataliya and Belinda Sloan. The Princess of Mirrus gave Konstantin a shocked look while Emma's mother blushed, like his small PDA embarrassed her.

But Emma? Tilted her head back and smiled up at him. "I'm having a wonderful time. Everyone is so kind."

"Of course they are kind. You are so sweet, to be unkind to you would be anathema."

"You might be exaggerating, but that's okay. I like it."

"You said you loved me," he blurted out with a complete lack of aplomb.

The sound of his younger brother groaning behind him told Konstantin that Dima had heard too. "Way to sound desperate, Konstantin."

Emma just smiled. "I did."

"Did you mean it?"

Emma turned in his arms, so their gazes met and no one else could intrude on this moment. "Yes, Kon. I meant it. I love you. With everything in me."

"That is why you forgave me."

"It is part of it."

"What is the other part?"

"I realized you loved me too and breaking up with me tore your heart into pieces just like it did mine."

"I'm not sure this is the best venue for this discussion," Nataliya tried to interject.

But Konstantin was enthralled by the expression in his wife's beautiful blue eyes. They were filled with understanding and yes, love.

"I do love you," he told her, needing to give her the words.

"I told you they loved each other," Mickey piped up, having come up with both his grandfathers in tow.

Everyone laughed except Emma and Konstantin.

He was too choked up to laugh or speak. She dropped her head against his chest. "I pictured you saying those words so many times, but maybe not in front of a bazillion people for the first time."

"I am not ashamed of my feelings," he assured her.

"That's a given," someone said, followed by more laughter.

"I think he should kiss her," Mickey opined.

Konstantin thought his son's idea was brilliant and proceeded to do just that.

Emma's wedding night was everything she could have ever dreamed it would be and then some. Saying "I love you" turned out to be a huge erotic trigger for her husband and they got very little sleep and a surfeit of pleasure.

Because neither of them seemed capable of stopping saying it.

And that was all right.

Emma would rather drown in the sentiment than ever live another day without it.

Kon made it clear he felt the same. She didn't think they were ever going to have a typical royal marriage, but they sure would have an adventurous one filled with love.

* * * * *

If you loved
His Majesty's Hidden Heir,
you're sure to enjoy the first instalment in the
Princesses by Royal Decree trilogy,
Queen by Royal Appointment.

Make sure to look out for
the final instalment in the series!
In the meantime, why not read one of these other
Lucy Monroe stories?

An Heiress for His Empire
A Virgin for His Prize
Kostas's Convenient Bride
The Spaniard's Pleasurable Vengeance
After the Billionaire's Wedding Vows…

Available now!

WE HOPE YOU ENJOYED
THIS BOOK FROM
⟨H⟩ HARLEQUIN
PRESENTS

Escape to exotic locations where passion knows no bounds.

Welcome to the glamorous lives of royals and billionaires, where passion knows no bounds. Be swept into a world of luxury, wealth and exotic locations.

8 NEW BOOKS AVAILABLE EVERY MONTH!

#3961 CROWNED FOR HIS CHRISTMAS BABY
Pregnant Princesses
by Maisey Yates
After being swept up in Prince Vincenzo's revenge plans, Eloise is carrying his surprise heir. And the man who vowed never to marry is claiming her—as his royal Christmas bride!

#3962 THE GREEK SECRET SHE CARRIES
The Diamond Inheritance
by Pippa Roscoe
Months after their passionate fling, rumors bring enigmatic Theron to Summer's doorstep—to discover a pregnancy as obvious as the still-sizzling desire between them! He will give their child the family unit he lost. But Summer's trust isn't so easily won...

#3963 DESERT KING'S SURPRISE LOVE-CHILD
by Cathy Williams
When King Abbas was forced to assume the role of ruler, he was forced to walk away from Georgie. Chance reunites them, and he learns two things: she's still utterly enchanting and *he's* a father!

#3964 THE CHRISTMAS SHE MARRIED THE PLAYBOY
Christmas with a Billionaire
by Louise Fuller
To save her pristine image from scandal, Santina must marry notorious playboy Louis. But after a past betrayal, it's not gossip she fears...it's the burning attraction that will make resisting her convenient husband impossible.

#3965 A CONTRACT FOR HIS RUNAWAY BRIDE
The Scandalous Campbell Sisters
by Melanie Milburne

Elodie needs billion-dollar backing to make a success of her fashion brand. As if pitching to a billionaire wasn't hard enough, Lincoln Lancaster is her ex-fiancé! He'll help her, but his deal has one condition: she'll finally meet him at the altar...

#3966 RECLAIMED FOR HIS ROYAL BED
by Maya Blake

Having tracked Delphine down, King Lucca can finally lay his family's scandalous past to rest...if she agrees to play the golden couple in public. And once again set alight by his touch, will Delphine reveal the explosive reason why she left?

#3967 THE INNOCENT'S PROTECTOR IN PARADISE
by Annie West

Tycoon Niall is the only person Lola can turn to when her life is threatened. He immediately offers her a hiding place—his private Gold Coast retreat! He's utterly off-limits, but their fierce desire incinerates any resistance...

#3968 THE BILLIONAIRE WITHOUT RULES
Lost Sons of Argentina
by Lucy King

Billionaire Max plays by his own rules, but there's one person that stands between him and the truth of his birth: tantalizingly tenacious private investigator Alex. And she's demanding they do things her way!

YOU CAN FIND MORE INFORMATION ON UPCOMING HARLEQUIN TITLES, FREE EXCERPTS AND MORE AT HARLEQUIN.COM.

HPCNMRB1121

*Elodie needs billion-dollar backing to make a success
of her fashion brand. As if pitching to a billionaire
wasn't hard enough, Lincoln Lancaster is her ex-fiancé!
He'll help her, but his deal has one condition: she'll
finally meet him at the altar…*

*Read on for a sneak preview of debut author
Melanie Milburne's next story for Harlequin Presents,
A Contract for His Runaway Bride.*

"Could you give me an update on when Mr. Smith will be available?"

The receptionist's answering smile was polite but formal. "I apologize for the delay. He'll be with you shortly."

"Look, my appointment was—"

"I understand, Ms Campbell. But he's a very busy man. He's made a special gap in his schedule for you. He's not usually so accommodating. You must've made a big impression on him."

"I haven't even met him. All I know is I was instructed to be here close to thirty minutes ago for a meeting with a Mr. Smith to discuss finance. I've been given no other details."

The receptionist glanced at the intercom console, where a small green light was flashing. She looked up again at Elodie with the same polite smile. "Thank you for being so patient. Mr.…erm… Smith will see you now. Please go through. It's the third door on the right. The corner office."

The corner office boded well—that meant he was the head honcho. The big bucks began and stopped with him. Elodie came to the door and took a deep, calming breath, but it did nothing to